TERRACE STORY

TERRACE STORY

STORY

A Novel

HILARY LEICHTER

ecco

An Imprint of HarperCollinsPublishers

TERRACE STORY. Copyright © 2023 by Hilary Leichter. All rights reserved. Printed in the United States of America. No part of this book may be used or reproduced in any manner whatsoever without written permission except in the case of brief quotations embodied in critical articles and reviews. For information, address HarperCollins Publishers, 195 Broadway, New York, NY 10007.

HarperCollins books may be purchased for educational, business, or sales promotional use. For information, please email the Special Markets Department at SPsales@harpercollins.com.

Ecco® and HarperCollins® are trademarks of HarperCollins Publishers.

FIRST EDITION

Designed by Alison Bloomer
Title Page Illustration © Arelix / Shutterstock

Library of Congress Cataloging-in-Publication Data has been applied for.
ISBN 978-0-06-326581-3

23 24 25 26 27 LBC 5 4 3 2 1

For Matt

Measure what can be measured, and make measurable what cannot be measured.

—GALILEO

"Well, we must wait for the future to show," said Mr Bankes, coming in from the terrace.

—VIRGINIA WOOLF, *To the Lighthouse*

TERRACE
STORY

TERRACE

—

THE OLD WINDOW GAVE A GRAND VIEW OF YELLOW TREE, trunk to branch. They called it Yellow Tree even though the ginkgo was yellow for only about a week each year, its fan-shaped leaves rustling to the ground at the first suggestion of a breeze. Annie and Edward held the baby to the window and said, "See? Yellow!" But she was too small to say "yellow" in response. She just looked and watched and touched the glass. They wiped her fingerprints from the window and kissed the fingers that made the prints. Then the leaves fell, and the scenery changed. Some views show less than half of what needs seeing.

When the rent became unpayable, they went in search of a more affordable living situation. *What's your living situation?* Annie turned the phrase over in her mind, the situation of their life. They had not saved nearly enough for a broker's fee, let alone a security deposit.

"It looks smaller than it really is," Edward said, leading Annie around the new apartment. A dimly lit lopsided square. "Give it some time, it might grow on you!"

"You mean it might literally grow?" Annie asked.

At the new apartment, there were no views of Yellow Tree. The introverted windows were gated and clasped and huddled around a central shaft that Edward dubbed

Pigeon Tunnel. Edward and Annie liked inventing proper nouns for their world. Yellow Tree, Pigeon Tunnel, Closet Mystery. Closet Mystery was Annie's term for the mystery of their single, overstuffed closet. Upon opening, what would catapult forth? It was a bona fide enigma. Edward and Annie picked a proper noun for their baby too. Her noun was Rose.

Annie strapped Rose to her chest while she unpacked, stuffing diapers and deconstructed boxes into Closet Mystery, keeping an arm around her, holding tight, in case the fabric of the sling happened to unfurl like a scarf in a gust of wind, loosing the baby onto the ground.

"Careful," she said to no one but herself.

Someday, Edward said, they would have a bit of outdoors all their own. A square of grass for playtime, a pot for planting herbs. They had said that at their last apartment too, and at the apartment before that, and they continued to say it even still, though perhaps with less conviction. They were cramped, Edward said, but in a way that felt familiar and warm, no? Yes, Annie agreed. Secretly, she felt that their lack of space probably signaled her lack of promise, a final judgment on her poor priorities and half-hewn choices. But it was a judgment that, in her deepest heart, had grown commonplace and comfortable, only jabbing its elbow of discontent at moments that found her particularly low. They were lucky in so many ways. They were healthy and happy and fine. They had spent every penny saved on moving in and moving out, even the coins from under the sink. Now there was a new sink, and an empty jar for fresh, shiny coins.

The building was closer to Edward's work, which offered day care. When Annie's unpaid maternity leave ended, she took the bus to her office and met Stephanie on the steps outside. Stephanie had covered Annie's clients while she was away.

"The prodigal mother returns!" Stephanie said.

"Where's my marching band?" Annie asked.

"Oh, the drum majorettes are upstairs. But wouldn't you know it, the flute section is out pregnant."

"All of them?"

"Toutes des flûtes," Stephanie said.

Stephanie walked Annie through the lobby and guided her from floor to floor, which Annie found strange, until she realized her keycard had been deactivated while she was away. They visited reception to get a new one.

"Let's have lunch today," Stephanie said. "I see a pastry in my future."

"Hey, did they move the copy machine?" Annie asked.

"No, they moved your desk."

They ate BLTs with bags of chips and talked about the reshuffling of the marketing team; the new, luxe chairs in the conference room; the water fountain that was still out of order. Annie was looking for an update on her clients, some distress call that signaled she was still needed.

"What can I say?" Stephanie said. "You missed nothing."

"Come over for dinner one night, why don't you?" Annie said.

"Oh no, no," Stephanie said. "I don't want to get in the way."

"Get in the way. We need to assemble our table. You can be the excuse."

Annie came home and told Edward they needed to buy a table. They put it on the credit card. Annie cut cloth napkins from old fabric, laid out the glasses, the forks, the recently unpacked dishes from her grandmother, each plate painted with a tiny gold animal.

"I brought wine!" Stephanie said, shoving through the front door and shaking Edward's hand. "Oh, and who on earth are you?" she asked Rose. Rose responded by handing Stephanie a toy.

Annie's first instinct was to explain the size of their new home. The neighborhood, his office, the day care, what a steal! And then she would nudge Edward to apologize for the lack of space, so cramped, the amicable kind of cramped, the colorful balls and bags and dolls on the floor.

But it was Stephanie who spoke first. She said, "Should we eat outside? It's such a beautiful night."

She opened the door that normally led to their closet and revealed a terrace, decorated with strings of twinkling lights. Knotted vines gathered around the edges, forking and blooming and racing up the sides of the apartment.

The terrace was news to Annie, and also news to Edward. Had they simply overlooked it this whole time? No, it wasn't possible.

"What?" Annie said under her breath. She settled Rose against her hip and peered out onto this terrace (her terrace?), which was equipped with a table and four chairs, a grill, and the kind of sturdy umbrella one could shove open on a sunny afternoon. Everything looked glossy and expensive, as if just purchased or just invented. She felt like she had found a missing pair of glasses sitting on top of her head.

"Closet Mystery indeed," Edward said, coming up behind her.

"Real Estate Mystery," Annie whispered. They looked at each other and walked through the terrace door at the same moment. (That's how big the door! That's how large the terrace!) They were unharmed, unchanged, and caught in the embrace of a warm autumn evening.

Stephanie was admiring a view that did not match the position of the apartment. No sight of Pigeon Tunnel, not anywhere. Straight ahead, they could see the remnants of a sunset, even though their side of the building faced east. Stephanie did not seem to notice the faulty geography.

"Shit, what a great space," she said.

"Imagine our luck!" Annie said, bringing forth the wine.

They sat on the terrace for hours, refilling their glasses and plates. In fact, the longer they stayed on the terrace, the more solid it felt underfoot. Edward let Rose fall asleep in his lap and kept her there for fear of waking her when standing. There was a sharp tension, followed by a sense of overwhelming calm. The two emotions alternated for Annie until both expired and were replaced with the achy, snoozy joy of a morning spent running around a playground. It was an outdoor kind of joy. She could certainly move her arms and legs, but she chose not to. They were weighed down and happy. Oh, and the way the breeze felt on her forehead, the way it brought a soft campfire smell up and over her face.

At the end of the night, Stephanie helped them carry the dishes and utensils to the kitchen, and they showed her down to the street.

"What fun. Especially this girlie," Stephanie said, tugging at Rose's foot.

"Thanks for making the trip," Edward said.

"Next time, you come to me!"

"Of course we will," Annie said, wrapping Stephanie in a hug. She couldn't wait to have the terrace all to herself, alone with Edward, with Rose, her family. She thought maybe they would sleep outside that night. How wild! Just to prove it was real.

When they had made it back upstairs to their apartment, the terrace was gone.

Annie opened the closet door and closed it, over and over, hoping for the kind of outcome that had already lodged itself beyond reach.

"Maybe it only appears when we entertain guests," Annie said.

"Or maybe it was just this one magic time!" Edward said, tossing his jeans in a pile on the floor, next to the crib, next to the stove, next to the table, for which they really did not have enough space, neither in the apartment nor on the credit card. "Tonight was the best," he said. "Tonight we had a terrace. We'll talk about it forever."

"Still," Annie said into the pillow.

"Still," Edward agreed.

Edward and Annie never went to Stephanie's home for dinner, because she did not invite them. Instead, they invited over family friends, their old neighbors, their roommates from college. They had a nice time catching up with all the people in their lives, introducing them to Rose, hearing their current stories. But there was no terrace with Dan and Patricia, not with the O'Neills, and not with Liza and Sunny. For each visit, Annie would set the table in just the same arrangement, with a mug of pollen-shedding flowers and the collection of gold animal plates, and then she would try to reveal the terrace. Instead of releasing the glow from a setting sun, the closet would cough up a stray bag of diapers.

"Maybe you have to turn the knob a certain way," Annie said, trying her hand at terrace sorcery. "Maybe it's all in the wrist."

The proper noun for this period was, as Edward put it, Sadness Home.

Annie wandered the apartment in a state of perpetual frustration, Rose hanging from her breast, the dishes gathering in the sink. She even missed a couple days of work. She dug through the mess of Closet Mystery and pressed her hands against the back wall, looking for a trapdoor or secret hinge.

She woke up early to feed Rose and paced the kitchen, imagining that the terrace might be tethered to cycles of the moon. Or perhaps the apartment was haunted by the terrace, an unruly architectural ghost that only visited when disturbed. Rose, for her part, did not seem troubled by her surroundings. She was still too young to be enchanted by a magic terrace, and perhaps Annie was too old. Annie looked into her daughter's eyes and almost remembered the magnitude of their puny, gorgeous life. But she slid across the surface of the thought, into a new and compelling theory. Rose reached for her mother's collar and stretched it wide.

What if there's only a terrace when Stephanie is here? Annie wondered.

She was right, of course. When Stephanie returned for a Sunday brunch, the terrace returned too. It was resplendent in the afternoon sun, the wooden slats dappled with light and strewn with acorns, gold and orange leaves underfoot. Annie didn't expect that you could yearn for a place so terribly after visiting it only once. There were other places she missed, treasured territories lifted off the earth, shuttered, gone. But the terrace arrived upon her with the relief of a long-awaited reunion. Annie felt a chill, because it was a reunion with herself. She had been accommodating some unknown injury for years, and it had silently joined the daily landscape of known feeling. Now, standing on the terrace, she woke to find her forgotten wound healed.

"You guys need a good sweep, huh?" Stephanie teased, kicking some leaves through the bars of the terrace and watching them float down to the street.

They spent the whole afternoon outside, plying Stephanie with drinks and snacks, and boards of cheese, and then a giant mug of steaming cider.

"I'm never leaving," Stephanie said, her overlarge sunglasses lolling down the bridge of her nose.

"Fine by me!" Annie said. She spread a blanket on the terrace floor and sat with Rose in her lap, the lip of the umbrella creating a perfect wedge of shade. They played with the plush pig, and Rose chewed on the corners of a book made from crinkly fabric. Edward grilled hot dogs and tightened the screws on the terrace chairs, entertaining Stephanie with stories about things that had never happened. Vacations they had not taken, friends they'd never had, the fortune they'd inherited from Annie's grandmother, when really all they had inherited was her set of gold animal plates.

"Just like that time when you and Edward were in Italy!" Stephanie said one day in the office, and Annie had to remind herself: they had never been to Italy.

Annie and Edward called these Terrace Stories, because when you are in a place that does not really exist, you can populate it with as many fables and legends as you like.

"I will never lie to you on solid ground," Edward said, and Annie knew it was true.

Yellow Tree, Pigeon Tunnel, Terrace Story.

Every weekend, Annie invited Stephanie for a visit.

"Maybe I can pop by for a minute," Stephanie would say, but it was never just a minute. They played Scrabble and chess, and they knit scarves and read books in the sun. They had picnic lunches and picnic dinners, and a picnic breakfast at dawn. Annie purchased some flowers and flowerpots and potting soil, for the perimeter of the terrace. She put it all on the credit card. Stephanie helped her nestle the mums in mounds of dirt.

"We can't keep forcing her to come over here," Edward said under his breath.

"Who's forcing?" Annie whispered. "I barely need to suggest it. She practically invites herself."

"But what's in it for her?" Edward asked. "I mean besides the terrace."

"Rosie, you're so stinky!" Stephanie said on the other side of the umbrella, holding the baby up in the air, too high, much too high, too near the edge.

"Careful, careful, careful," Annie shouted, and ran to take Rose and change her.

"Oh, boo-hoo," Stephanie mock cried. But for a moment, Annie noticed real sadness along the edges of Stephanie's voice and tried to locate what kind of space those edges indicated, how that space wanted to fill itself. If there was a yearning, Annie could not tell what the yearning was for. She looked back at Stephanie and

Stephanie met her gaze, holding Annie's attention for a moment too long. Really, who was this stranger in her home?

Stephanie walked to the terrace door and blocked the entrance, shouted, "Hey, Eddie, you got another beer for me?"

They stayed up playing charades and laughed so hard they thought the terrace would fall straight down through the center of the earth. The toilet was broken again, and this time they would have to call a plumber, a real plumber, not simply a friend who owed a favor. But for the time being, just once, Edward turned his back to the ladies and peed off the edge of the terrace. They howled with laughter.

"Annie's going to start stocking up on diapers for you, Eddie!" Stephanie roared, leaning too far back in her chair.

Annie and Edward fell asleep without cleaning up the terrace, but the terrace cleaned itself. Stephanie came over on a rainy Saturday, and it sparkled in the drizzle, no beer bottles or napkins, no trash to be found. The mums were growing large and lush.

At the office, Annie's supervisor moved her desk to a different floor and redistributed some of her clients to Stephanie, just for convenience. *She's more up to date on everything,* the email said. *Be the team player we all know and adore!*

"Do your coworkers adore you?" Annie asked Edward.

"Hey now," Edward said, "is this a Terrace Story?"

"I was thinking maybe Stephanie could bring a friend when she comes over this weekend. What do you think?" Annie shoved a tower of toilet paper into the closet.

"Great idea. I adore it."

Annie texted Stephanie, making the invite. *Bring a friend? Or maybe more than a friend,* she added, dot dot dot.

Stephanie came by herself, carrying a board game. The dice and tiny plastic parts tumbled around the box with a rattle, the type of messy noise that lets everyone know important pieces are missing.

"Just you?" Annie asked.

"Just me," Stephanie said, and went to sit next to Edward.

One night, Annie pulled the record player out onto the terrace, stringing its cords back through the apartment. The three of them danced and took turns waltzing with Rose, holding her up and wiggling her legs, but never throwing her in the air, not like this, not so high, not outside.

When they were completely out of breath and tired of being on their feet, Edward told a Terrace Story. Later, it would be the only one that Annie would remember from start to finish. It was about a date that they had never had, with a limousine they had never hired, and a cheesy bouquet of roses they had never purchased. And that's how they came up with the name Rose, in the context of this Terrace Story. In the context of real life, Rose was Annie's grandmother's name. Annie did not appreciate this small revision.

"This restaurant," Edward said, "it's the kind of place

with private dining, where you get to sit in your own room, a room with just one table and two chairs. And the waiters knock on the private door before bringing the food, the drinks, the bill. They even knock before entering to ask, 'Would you like to have dessert?'"

"But how many times do they knock?" Stephanie asked. "Is it a rat-a-tat-a-tat?"

"No," Edward said. "It's more of a syncopated triplet."

Stephanie tried to tap out a triplet but started laughing.

"Shave and a haircut, plus two bits," Edward said.

"Special delivery!"

Annie twitched. It was all so playful. It was an inside joke, and she was on the outside. The Terrace Stories were meant for Edward and Annie, but here they were, tapping their secret codes on the terrace rail. And there was the look on Stephanie's face, like she knew the whole story by heart. Why a private room, Annie thought, unless you don't want to be seen?

"That was a real date," Annie said. "A real date you went on with someone else."

They were throwing off their clothing and throwing off their shoes. It was late. Stephanie was gone, and so was the terrace.

"What are you talking about?" Edward said.

"That wasn't a Terrace Story. It was a real story."

"That's absurd."

"Don't lie. I mean, the whole bit with the knocking!"

"Annie, come here. Stop now. Come here. It wasn't real."

They lay as far apart in the bed as possible, which of course was not very far. Then Edward's heel wedged itself between Annie's ankles, and soon they were hugging, and soon everything was on its way to better.

Annie woke up to feed Rose, and she checked the credit card statements. She looked for a restaurant charge. She looked for a limousine or a place in their neighborhood with private dining rooms. There wasn't anything logical about how she felt, and yet, can the woman who visits an imaginary terrace really claim logic for herself? Even if the story about the date wasn't real, Edward had made it real by telling it, and now the false story was part of their living situation, like a fresh growth on the side of a plant, like the terrace.

She fell asleep nursing and dreamed that Edward apologized in exactly the right way. I dreamed you would say that, and then you did, she said in the dream. But the apology instantly corroded as it was spoken, because Annie knew without waking that all his words were actually her own.

Edward stumbled out of bed and found her in the chair. "Maybe it was a real date I *wanted* to go on, someday," he said. "With you."

STEPHANIE JOINED THEM for Thanksgiving. The weather had stayed warm, and so of course they ate outside. Annie had tried to purchase a turkey, but the credit card was declined. She had to carry the turkey all the way back through the store to the last aisle. Edward burst into action, stirring and mashing, declaring their dinner the Meal of Sides. They feasted on supplementary dishes, which, Stephanie insisted, were the best part anyway.

"I love a good stuffing!" she said to Edward, throwing broken bread crusts in the pan.

Rose stuck her fingers in the potatoes and wore a pumpkin onesie that Annie had picked out special.

And New Year's Eve, with the weather still just right for sweaters, they gathered on the terrace with mugs of bad champagne. Thanks to the altered view, their party could see large, blossoming willows of fireworks in the distance. These were the ones that Annie remembered from her childhood, her grandmother taking her to the local park to see the flowering gowns of twinkling white lights, opening, falling, and disappearing through the dark.

"If you celebrate the New Year on an imaginary terrace," Edward whispered to Annie, "does it really happen?"

"It all really happens," Annie said, smiling up at Edward.

When the minutes turned to seconds, and the seconds concluded their downward march, Edward turned to Stephanie and kissed her on the cheek, perhaps so she would not feel left in the cold. Annie took Rose up in her arms and kissed her all over her face, planted a raspberry on her stomach. Then Stephanie reached for Rose, as a kindness, so that Edward could move for Annie's lips, which he did, but once again, Stephanie brought Rose

much too close to the edge of the terrace, much too close
for Annie to bear, and she grabbed Rose back from Stephanie without waiting for Edward's embrace. The physical-
ity of the moment passed quickly, but it lingered from the
end of one year into the beginning of the next, Annie and
Edward standing only steps apart, the queasy sensation of
extra distance tucked between the inches.

In early winter, they bundled Rose from head to tiny
toe and plopped her on the terrace floor. She could now
sit up without support, her hands slapping her thighs, mit-
tened and buttoned.

"She looks so much like both of you," Stephanie said,
as if making a concession. She was building a snowman
at the edge of the terrace, embellishing his face with perfectly ripe vegetables that Annie had planned on cooking
into a stew for dinner.

"How should I do his eyes, Rosie?" Stephanie said,
laughing.

Annie would retrieve the vegetables when Stephanie
wasn't looking, she decided. The cold would keep them
usable for dinner, surely. The snow was still fresh. The
carrots would need to be washed and peeled, diced, but
otherwise, fine. Then Stephanie knocked the bundle of
carrots over the edge of the terrace.

"Whoops! Man down," she said. "Should I run and
grab them?"

"Don't bother," Annie said. Where, exactly, would
Stephanie run? And where, at what haunted perimeter,
would she end up?

On a frigid Monday, Annie had a meeting scheduled with her supervisor. She planned on asking about pursuing additional clients, to make up for the redistributed list. She planned on asking for a raise.

Instead, they suggested shifting Annie to a part-time schedule. We can only afford to keep you on for these days, at this rate, her supervisor said. Especially with Stephanie taking most of your clients. You are always welcome to find something else, if this doesn't meet your needs, and so forth.

Annie decided that the job no longer met her needs.

To be honest, you've seemed distracted, the final email said.

She packed her plant and pictures and pens in a box, and ran into Stephanie near the elevator bank.

"Oh, it's you," Annie said. Stephanie was always popping into view, as familiar as any of the furniture in her home.

"I just heard," Stephanie said. "Listen. I'm so sorry. It wasn't my—"

"It's fine. Are you leaving now?"

"Yeah, I was just about to head out."

"You should come over," Annie said.

"Really? Right now?"

"Now," Annie said, holding the door.

Standing in the elevator with Stephanie was the opposite of standing on the terrace. Annie could feel their heat, their silence contained and amplified and spun in circles. She wanted to bang on the walls or smack the emergency button, her eyes welling with an unexpected rage. She wanted one of them to be somewhere else but felt they were doomed to always be in the same place at the same time. She caught Stephanie staring at her from the other side of the elevator with a rude sort of curiosity and resisted the urge to swat her away. She needed for Stephanie to come to her home, reach out her hand, open the closet door, and everything would resolve, her anger sizzling off the sides of the terrace. But hadn't Annie sometimes felt angry on the terrace too? Hadn't she felt something worse than anger?

"Can I carry your box?" Stephanie asked.

"No," Annie said.

When they arrived at the apartment, Edward was feeding Rose and warming up leftovers for himself.

"Oh! I wish you had called first," he said, motioning to Stephanie.

"It's fine," Annie said, trying to remain calm. All she wanted to do was relax and feel that lazy kind of joy, the happy weight on her legs and arms. "Let's go sit outside."

"I don't know," Stephanie said, halfway out of her coat. "It's below freezing."

"Who cares? We have blankets. We'll drink hot tea!" Annie exclaimed, throwing her box of office goods down near the closet door.

"It's ten degrees outside," Edward said. He looked at the box and then at his wife.

"Can't we stay inside?" Stephanie asked. "We can watch a movie. Cozy, cozy." She shifted her weight from one leg to the other, looking uneasy, and, for the first time, unwelcome.

"I don't know," Annie said. She felt an outrageous despair rising inside her, that jab of discontent, hitting harder and sharper every time Stephanie opened her mouth to speak. She took Rose up in her arms. "I don't know, on second thought, maybe you should just leave."

"Annie, if this is about work—"

"Stephanie, don't go," Edward said. "It's really fine!" He scrambled toward Stephanie, trying to make sense of the moment, probably terrified that Annie would say something awful to her, Annie figured, something that would reveal the way they had used Stephanie ill, taken advantage, negotiated her friendship for a bit of outdoors. Or worse, perhaps his desire that Stephanie should stay was a genuine one. Perhaps he felt (and this word fell like an unhitched icicle) a *fondness* for her. The pain of that delicate noun was more powerful and precise than the amorphous rage Annie had carried home from the office, and it stunned her into cooperation.

"Sorry," Annie said, shaking her head. "I'm so sorry. I'm not myself. Of course we can stay inside. We can watch a movie." She offered Edward a faint, confused smile. Her anger was still there, but a sudden exhaustion had buried it several layers deep. This was the way sadness often arrived in Annie's life, an unexpected density of feeling that freighted every other emotion until the only thing left was fatigue.

Stephanie gave a look to Edward and put out her hand;

mouthed, *It's fine;* gathered her scarf; and walked to the door. Annie tried to imagine Stephanie returning home to her own apartment and realized she could not picture it. She still had not been invited to visit.

"See you later, sweet Rosie," Stephanie said.

The nickname burrowed under Annie's skin and did not leave. Before Annie had turned ten and was taken to live with her grandmother, she was just Anne. Nouns can change once, and then change forever, all thanks to a small addition.

THEY HAD GONE weeks without Stephanie, but it was not until early March, when snow started melting down the windows, that Annie fully felt the loss of the terrace. With her new free time, she went for long walks with Rose buckled in the stroller. They ambled through the neighborhood, sampling the occasional discount dough-nut and coffee, Rose grabbing at the drops of water that trickled from branches, vocalizing with the birds. Annie tried to avoid crushing the earthworms, but occasionally, one worm was bound to split in two. And then their walk would end, and home again, there were no exits or en-trances to safely throw open, no extra air or space to claim. She didn't feel trapped, but it had been easier to bear the boundaries of her home before she'd known the terrace.

She marked the days with Rose's milestones, which accumulated at an alarming rate: Laugh, Crawl, Food,

Wave, Word. These were the new proper nouns in her life, all firsts. She marked them down in a book of firsts and dreamed about the other nouns to come. Even the ones that weren't firsts or lasts were exciting. The middle would be just as good, or even the best, like the center slice cut from a square cake.

Despite the terrifying, mounting expense of Annie's unemployment, Edward seemed resigned to the new arrangement, even happy. He encouraged her to take her time, as much time as she wanted. Not too much, you know, just the right amount, as long as the right amount was the amount she needed. He never mentioned Stephanie, at least, not until the day she rang their bell.

That morning, the temperature climbed to what would have been ideal terrace weather. It was truly spring, the spring they remembered from childhood, the kind that was always anticipated, even if it so rarely emerged. The birds had made their nest on the window ledge in Pigeon Tunnel, and the pigeon eggs did not provoke disgust in Annie, nor tenderness, but rather a sort of sustained curiosity. She checked on them every morning. She was checking the eggs when Stephanie arrived.

"Can I come in?" Stephanie asked, carrying what looked like a pan of homemade brownies.

"Of course," Annie said. But why of course? Some animal tendency unveiled itself within her, and she bared her teeth. After a moment, she could play it off as a smile, and she did.

"Should I take off my shoes?" Stephanie asked. It was an absurd thing to say, after the many months she had spent stomping through their home in heels and boots and flats alike. But perhaps their home had changed. Perhaps Stephanie had changed too.

Annie waved her hands, dismissing the question. "I'm glad you're here," she said, and immediately regretted it. Was she glad? She made way for Stephanie, for the brownies.

"Stephanie!" Edward said, coming from behind the counter with Rose nestled against his hip. "What a nice surprise."

Annie knew when her husband was surprised. She remembered his face from the evening of the terrace's first arrival, from his thirtieth birthday party, that joy-tinged ambush of family and friends; from the afternoon when she'd told him she was pregnant with Rose; from the day Rose was born, two weeks early; from the moment long ago when he'd discovered, despite all other possible outcomes, that he didn't just love Annie, but that she loved him too.

His current face, wide and warm, did not resemble those other incarnations of his face. No, not surprised at all. His eyebrows shot up with the smooth momentum of a well-oiled scheme.

"Let's go sit outside and talk," he said, leading Stephanie to the closet door. She took the knob in her hand as if she'd never been away, and with a slight rotation of the wrist, there was the terrace, just as they remembered it. The mums, despite the interceding months, continued to bloom. Annie had forgotten what it felt like to have the door open, the air rushing through their home, the light filtering the color of their floors with a richer hue. Her shoulders uncramped and the crick in her neck seemed to loosen. For a moment, she almost failed to recall how angry she was, how uncomfortable. What a relief, to have more, after having less.

"Did you invite her?" Annie asked Edward, once Stephanie was safely outside.

"Don't be cross," Edward said, shuffling Annie through the door and into the sunlight. He followed closely behind her, carrying Rose. "Please," he added.

They wandered around in silence for some moments, surveying the surroundings, taking in the terrace and its new season. In spring, they learned, the terrace smelled of dew and fresh flowers. Had the trees changed, Annie wondered, and been replaced with more fragrant versions, to best convey the current month? Of course, Stephanie did not know they had been bereft of their terrace, and so their puttering around must have seemed bizarre.

"Stephanie, would you like something to drink?" Annie asked.

"Oh no, thank you. I won't be staying long," she said. She waited until everyone was seated before speaking again. "I wanted to apologize, for intruding on your life, your work. I feel I probably made a complete nuisance of myself."

"Don't be ridiculous!" Edward said, and Annie watched him, watched her. Was this exchange rehearsed?

"I somehow couldn't help myself. I have trouble," Stephanie said, looking down, an oblique confession that, nevertheless, seemed honest.

"You're never a nuisance," Annie said, watching Edward again, and Edward made a motion with his chin, encouraging Annie to continue. "We've missed you. Rose has missed you." Annie took Rose onto her lap, as if to cancel the previous statement, laying unequivocal claim to the child. In mere moments, the sun had dried Rose's wet curls, turned them warm and soft. Annie buried her face in Rose's hair, lingering on the phrase *Rose has missed you*. There was something crucial here, but the crucial information darted away, refracting and escaping in the pleasant morning light. Stephanie watched Annie with great interest, as if this moment were the only one she had come to witness.

"Anyway," Stephanie said. "That's all I have to say. I've been so grateful for your hospitality."

And then, as if propelled by the terrace, in conjunction with the word *hospitality*, Annie jolted from her seat. "Stay a little longer," she said. "I'll go and plate those delicious brownies you brought."

She set Rose down in Stephanie's lap and lifted herself away, barely in control of her limbs, wondering if she had been speaking aloud or only in her head. Before long, she was in the kitchen. How did I get here? she thought. And where is Rose? She could hear the birdsong and the song of her family in the distance, their familysong, Rose cooing and producing sounds to accompany the planes overhead, her husband's laugh rising and then falling in its distinctive staccato.

"Babe, come back quick!" Edward said. "There's a flying squirrel! Aren't those extinct?"

Annie felt her heart pounding in her chest, a shortness of breath. She dropped the plate on the floor. She somehow knew she would never see the flying squirrel but did not yet know why it mattered.

Edward said, "Quick! You're missing it!"

When Annie turned around, Stephanie's body was fully blocking the doorway. She had a neutral expression on her face, or maybe it was slightly bemused. She closed the door halfway, the light dimming, a shadow falling on the floor. And then, she took hold of the knob as she had so many times before, only this time, from the outside. Stephanie clicked the door shut. The terrace, once again, was gone. Annie was alone.

IF IT IS ever possible to stop thinking of death, then Annie willed this for herself. In order to proceed, it was necessary to eliminate the threat of death from her thoughts. The exposure, the winters, the heat, the animals, the rain, the snow, the unknown. In order to proceed, Annie needed to make an assumption of life. It was under this assumption that she waited for Edward and Rose.

At first, the waiting was easy. Their return felt imminent. She waited with the assumption of life. Of course, there were the initial screams and the side-splitting moans, sounds that came from some nameless part of her body. But then, she waited. She observed the eggs of Pigeon Tunnel, ate the pan of brownies, sat on the floor near the closet. With great diligence, she tried to rotate her wrist at just the right speed, pulling the knob toward her and hoping to reveal Edward, smiling on the other side of the door.

Or was he Eddie now? Was their daughter Rosie?

Then the pigeon eggs were abandoned by their mother. Then they broke open without hatching, a thin skein of yellow rising from the shell of each egg. Then the eggs were snatched, eaten by other pigeons, and so the consideration of death always had a way of returning.

Annie moved from her spot next to the closet and huddled inside the closet itself. Proximity, she thought, will get the job done. Only a few days after that, she could hear their voices beyond the closet wall, or so she believed. Their familysong, pealing like bells just beyond reach. And of course, she could hear them more clearly when the closet was completely closed, so she tucked her knees to her chest and pulled the door shut.

She could have listened to them forever, sitting there, her head cushioned against their abandoned sweaters and puffy coats. Of course, she didn't. Grief is not the door that tucks you in; it's the door that shuts you out. But Annie allowed herself this moment. The plastic hangers above her head shifting with the weightlessness of wind chimes. The questions hardening and multiplying. What nouns will my daughter learn? What Terrace Stories will she tell? An imagined breeze from somewhere unseen. A proper name for this feeling, on the tip of Annie's tongue. The rest of the world receding slowly from view.

FOLLY

THE COUPLE FIRST SAW THE HOUSE FROM A GREAT DISTANCE.
They merged onto the highway and spotted it way off the shoulder, over the tops of trees, a crumbling majestic estate with brittle gardens and large empty windows.

"Are you sure that's it?" the man asked.

"I'm checking the map," the woman said. She piled her hair on top of her head, then let it drop around her shoulders. He loved when she did that.

"We should have followed the caravan from the cemetery," he said.

"You mean the procession."

"Parade?"

"Definitely not that," she said, laughing.

There had been a funeral that morning, and now they made their way toward a hosted brunch. The address was printed on a small cream-colored card, with a style of calligraphy Lydia especially liked. It was the type of thing she might've picked out herself. *Please join us for refreshments and remembrances.* She folded it several times into an accordion shape and slipped it in her pocket, then leaned over from the passenger side to rest her head on her husband's shoulder.

"Hey, be careful, I'm driving here." George swerved the car as a joke, and she flinched. He was always making jokes like this, with inscrutable punch lines. He was not a comedian; he was a historian. He specialized in the Middle Ages, which wasn't typically funny, though he claimed it had its moments.

"You're just hilarious," Lydia said, catching her breath.

George couldn't help himself. She was a delightful object of torment. She made it so easy for him. He put on his blinker and rejoined the right lane.

Maybe the punch line had to do with the fact that someday one of them would die.

"I'm going to ask Rose why she raised such an adorable backseat driver," George said.

"You will ask my mother nothing of the sort."

Outside, the cicadas were symphonic. The clouds rolled past their windshield in crumbling formations of limestone and pink quartz. The sky was one shade of blue with the windows up and another kind of blue when they were rolled down. Or was that a memory from a different car, on a different day?

They took the next exit and after a mile or two, there it was: a long, snaking driveway that opened onto a mansion of sorts. One of those paved entrances that could have been a moat in another era.

"Where are we?" Lydia asked, looking around.

"You have reached your destination," George said.

"But when are we?"

"Half past one."

"What century, I mean."

She smoothed out the fabric of his sleeve. He was still in his black suit. Lydia was wearing a beautifully tailored blazer, a thick charcoal tweed that she had worn to another funeral a long time ago. It still fit around the middle. After all, she was barely showing. She was puzzling over something but couldn't remember what. The question rotated inside her for a sustained moment, then dissolved like sugar in hot water.

The house was somehow larger and smaller than what she had imagined from the interstate. Which is another way of saying, she had been doubly wrong. Lydia thought about how the mind's eye can be inaccurate in both directions, leaving room and also not making quite enough. The body is much better at expanding, even though people are always claiming you can expand your mind with books or courses or concertos or a really good joint.

"A quaint little cottage, huh?" she said, and he kissed her ear.

It looked monstrous from the side but modest from the front. The bushes surrounding the door felt crisp to the touch. And there was a smell. Mulch? Putrefaction and the turning of soil, a landscaping project no doubt. The only welcoming aspect of the property was the row of cars parked along the street, signaling a gathering somewhere close by.

"Well, you've always liked rustic," George said.

"No, sir, I like retro," Lydia said, piling her hair on top of her head again.

"Retro, rustic, let's call the whole thing off," he sang.

"I love a ruin best of all."

"Yeah?"

"Mmm. And remember: where there is death, there are bagels. Come on," she said, taking his hand. They walked through the unlocked door to find a host, or a guest, or a friendly face. Ah yes, then the question returned. For the life of her, she could not remember who had died.

SOME TIME PASSED. George was holding a warm mug and looking at the framed photographs on the wall. His body must have been carefully arranged in this position; he could not remember lifting the mug nor filling it. His wife appeared by his side out of nowhere, as if from a mist. Dull murmurs and muffled sobs could be detected in a nearby room. She held out a plate of deli salads, crackers, miniature toasts, fruit, a bialy with schmear. This was something he loved about their marriage, the shared party plate. Once, at an event with gorgeous canapés and soufflé on tiny spoons, Lydia went foraging and brought a saucer filled with lime wedges back to their table, plus two cocktail forks. That wasn't their wedding, was it? It could have been.

"Something's not right with this place," she said.

He was about to agree, but low vibrations of music sounded from an upstairs floor, and he lost the thread.

Suddenly, the parlor. Lydia found herself standing over an etched crystal bowl of punch and a ladle engraved with a familiar monogram. Or maybe it was a store brand. The glasses were dainty and looked extrémely fragile. All around her people spoke in hushed tones. She couldn't quite catch anyone's eye. She somehow knew that the glassware had been purchased as a set and that one piece was missing. Sure enough, there were only eleven vessels where there should have been twelve. She went looking for George, to tell him about the missing cup, but he was nowhere to be found.

Then she realized the twelfth cup was in her hand.

"Does this have alcohol in it?" she asked a group of turned shoulders, gesturing at the punch, but no one responded directly. One sip wouldn't hurt the baby. It might even help, she thought, taking in the grim surroundings. Chilly. Everyone here was so rude. She thought of the old turn of phrase. *You look like you've seen a ghost!* Maybe they had. Now she was the one being rude.

Lydia's mind had wandered and so had her feet, landing her up on the other side of the estate, gazing into a bedroom. It was tastefully decorated, out of a catalog really, with chenille throws and pressed linen sheets. Her neck was hot, and she kept piling the curls on top of her head, only to let them fall back down again. A silly habit that drove George wild. She went to the dresser as if it were the most natural thing and rummaged for a hair clip.

"There you are," George said, falling back onto a

love seat in the corner of the room and pulling her into his lap.

"I got lost."

"You got nosy."

"So? You abandoned me," she said.

"Hardly. I'm the one who was left alone, bereft!"

They sat there for a moment together, looking out the window at the property, which was enormous and seemed to span a full county. There were stately trees that housed entire ecosystems, and farther in the distance, trellised gardens with wilted flowers. It could take you a whole lifetime to frolic through the grass here, if frolicking was your thing. Near the edge of the road, they could see the folly. A stone wreckage, like a medieval tower that had sunk below the surface of the earth, leaving only a cupola aboveground.

"What is that over there?" Lydia asked him, pointing.

"The folly? It's decorative."

"I mean what's it for?"

"Nothing, it's decorative," George said. "It doesn't have a purpose."

"It needs a life coach."

"Or a lover."

The folly was not so terribly far from the house, but through the window, it seemed to be in rapid retreat, fading into the scenery.

"Maybe we can go exploring?" he asked.

"After the eulogy," she said.

"They did the eulogy at the cemetery."

"Where oh where did my little mind go?"

"Let's find it," he said. "Should we tell them we're stepping outside?"

"Tell who?"

IT HAD TURNED into a hot autumn day, and Lydia molted her blazer along the path of the hike. Once they had arrived in the domed shade of the folly, she tested an overturned stone with her foot to make sure it didn't wobble, then sat down. All around her the light and leaves were gold and soft, and the beauty settled in her chest the way beauty often did, transitioning from something seen to something felt, something both remembered and experienced at the same time. Tucked above one of the cornices, she spotted a small doll, a colorful children's plaything with a lanyard dangling from its middle. Ivy and moss had grown around its edges, and it looked trapped in its little nest. Lydia had an impulse to bring the toy inside, but when she reached for it, her heart sank. Or maybe the baby kicked? She confused these two things quite a bit. Lydia stopped reaching and fanned herself dramatically with an outstretched hand.

"It's not that warm out, is it?" George said.

"Warmth is not empirical!"

"Of course it is."

"Well, clearly I am be-shvitzed over here, darling."

"Be-shvitzed, bo-thered, and bea-utiful," he sang.

"Do you remember," Lydia asked, "when autumn was chilly?"

George wiped her brow with the side of his sleeve, and she grinned, wiping the rest of her sweat on his chest, nuzzling into his belly and the soft meat of him that gave way for her affection. She left a round wet mark on his pressed shirt.

"Come on," he said, out of breath. "How in the fuck are we going to chase around a toddler if we can barely go for a walk?"

"Fee, fi, fo, fum. What folly!"

"I'm serious."

"Shall I steal a child from near the punch bowl," Lydia said, "and ask her to run for her life?"

"No. Race me instead."

George grinned at her with a playful meanness. He knew she could not turn down a contest. It did not matter what kind.

"I will do no such thing," she said, but she was already relacing her boots.

"Winner buys dinner?" he suggested, stretching his calves against a Doric column.

"No, we have the meat loaf defrosting," she said.

"Loser eats crow?" he said.

"Crows are nearly extinct, my love, try to be more sensitive."

"Fine. Winner gets to die first." Another one of his jokes.

"Terrific. How funereal!"

"I can read the room." Now George was doing exaggerated lunges and she couldn't help but laugh.

"Wait a minute," she said. "Doesn't winner want to live longest?" After saying it out loud, Lydia immediately knew she was wrong. Winner wants to live together, not alone.

"On your mark . . ."

"I'm not falling for this!" she shrieked, and ran back to the house without waiting for the countdown, knocking into George and squeezing out a narrow lead. He easily accelerated and lifted her up around her waist, which she called her Middle Ages.

"Let me go," she said. "I'm ancient history!"

He placed her down to the side of the path, then trotted forward. They had each cheated so as not to live without the other. But he had won.

On the drive home, it occurred to Lydia that they might've offended the bereaved with their silly game, but again, she could not quite put her finger on who was bereaved, or who had departed. The information fluttered against her face, too close to see but near enough to be a bother. If she couldn't remember whom she had offended, then she probably had not offended anyone. Right? No, that wasn't right. And yet. The mourners were a gray faceless cloud that tottered to the back of her consciousness, rarely to be considered again.

They had to stop many times so she could use the bathroom. Her bladder was infamous in those early months. At each rest area, George bought a souvenir and begged Lydia to save the knickknack for his impending funeral. She emerged from the ladies' room, and he held up a bright green mug that declared a certain state to be, in fact, for lovers.

"Oh, hello, I don't believe we've been introduced," she said to the mug. "How do you do."

"Bury us together," George said. "Please, dear, don't forget."

"I'll remember you and your lover fondly."

He accumulated a bag of candies, a key chain, and a bumper sticker that warned of BEARS CROSSING.

"My most prized possessions," he said.

After she agreed to bury George with his prizes, they moved on to the finer points, like speeches and songs. He didn't want anything fussy. Just a sixteen-piece orchestra.

"And you'll write something," he said. "What's your fee?"

"You can't afford me," Lydia said, sticking her nose in the air, but he absolutely could. She was very, very affordable.

It wasn't until later that night, in bed, when the idea of George's death landed differently. Her husband's death, which he had won fair and square. Lydia had not felt this pointless circle for some time, the unmistakable shape of dread, the Questions. She was in its circumference now. What kind of demise had they invited by playing their stupid game? Would George die young?

Was he still considered young, and more important, was she? She could be a blushing widow and old mom, both! Geriatric birth and geriatric death were two separate things, after all. She leaned over to make sure he was still breathing. Ah, he was snoring. The mediocre meat loaf from dinner sat funny in Lydia's stomach, but at least if she'd accidentally poisoned him, she'd also poisoned herself.

"Mommy brain," George said when she finally confessed her fear. She had been holding it in for weeks. He wasn't wrong about the hormones, but did he have to say it like that? Mommy brain, the mind expanding. For a moment Lydia wished him dead, and then she started to cry.

"I'm sorry. I just wished you were dead!"

"You're not that powerful, you know. You can't think me to death."

"Why not? I think myself to death all the time," she said into a tissue.

"That's true. But I'm not going anywhere."

"People drop dead every day," Lydia said. "We were just dressed in black for old so-and-so."

"Dressed in black for who?" George asked, which surprised her. She had hoped he would fill in the name. Now Lydia was even less certain about the funeral they had attended.

"People are dropping like flies," she said, swinging her hand around for effect. "It's the latest craze."

He laughed and wrapped his arms around her. "I thought flies were dropping like people."

"Only in Nevada," she said. "The scientists are looking into it."

"Would you like a rematch?" he asked. "I'll let you win this time."

"Don't be ridiculous," she said, but yes, really that was what she wanted more than anything. She did not want to outlive anyone, let alone him.

George returned to grading papers, and Lydia went back to writing an article about shrimp, and how they had been overfarmed, and how very soon there would be none left in any of the oceans. No scampi, no cocktail, no coconut. None whatsoever.

THINGS WERE BETTER then. Lydia had a bump the size of a novelty gumball machine. She had a chart that showed her how to measure. People were happy to see her wherever she went, and she was not used to this feeling, the ability to make strangers smile and look grateful for her presence. In this way, carrying a child was like being a child. The world opened its arms to you, whether you wanted it or not. And she couldn't worry about her husband dying when she was consumed with keeping a baby alive. All the books and tricks and whole grains, she had charts for those too. George was on a health kick of his own. He rode his bike to their birthing classes, to work, to the market. Once, he went to buy some necessities for dinner and took a long time coming home. His bike careened across Lydia's mind and straight into traffic, overwhelmed by the weight of the ginger ale and the family pack of chicken thighs. Before she could call him or send him a message, he was walking through the front door, as alive as anyone else, telling her about the long lines at the cash register. Lydia pretended that everything was fine, and pretending was almost the real thing.

On certain nights, she found herself dreaming of the folly, especially in the third trimester. At the end of the dream, an earthquake split the grounds apart, and the folly gave way to reveal a fully interred fortress, with burrowed parapets and towers, rising to greet the sky from the dust and rubble. It had been a castle all along. She hoped that when she died, they buried her all the way down, nothing left poking out aboveground, for god's sake. But who would be there to bury her if he died first? Oh, right. She touched her belly.

George was working with his students on their dissertations. The Venerable Bede, the bubonic plague, ten different approaches to the Crusades. Lydia was calmer than before but still prone to outbursts. When he did not show up for a sonogram, she called him thirty times. Dead on the side of the road. Dead under the heel of a villain! Hog-tied to the train tracks, like in the cartoons. No, he had been caught up at work, didn't she understand? Yes, he was caught up at work with the very pretty graduate student, but nothing had happened. They were just reviewing for a presentation. He wondered why Lydia couldn't worry about infidelity, like a normal person. Every story had to end in his death. Couldn't she let him die at his own pace, in peace?

"You're stealing my thunder," George said. Lydia was sobbing over some bread sticks because he had been away from his phone all day. "When I die, I want to really surprise your socks off!"

"That's not funny," she said, pressing her runny nose into his neck.

"It's hilarious," he said. "Think of how cold your feet will be."

"You're cruel."

He carried her into the bedroom and pulled down her pants, moving his hands under each leg, tracing her skin with the tips of his fingers. She sighed. With his head between her knees, there was very little worry about death.

"Please. Don't be an English major," he said, before she could find the pun.

Then afterward, he read the latest journals and scholarship while Lydia slept next to him. It's not that he thought he would be able to survive without her. But sometimes he thought that perhaps she was less likely to survive without him. It was an ungenerous feeling, but that didn't make it untrue. A stingy little fact, taking shape, bending and twisting his heart in unexpected ways. He envied his graduate students who still believed themselves to be immortal. Nothing could shake the invincible realities they inhabited. Their worlds were unending. The pretty graduate student spoke in whens, never ifs. When I get tenure, she said, when I have children, when I travel. When I'm older. When I'm old. When you're long gone, she meant.

THERE WAS THE extinction of shrimp, then trout and salmon, and at last, the aforementioned crows. Lydia's work kept her busy. She was halfway through writing a long-form piece on the inevitable loss of snails when she started having contractions.

"I'll call the doctor," George said.

"Call my editor first."

The line was busy, and then they were on hold, and then the nurse begged them to wait a little longer.

"Snail's pace indeed!" George said.

"Everyone," the nurse said, "I mean *everyone*, is having a baby today."

Oh, Lydia hated that she was doing something popular. Then again, extinction had to start somewhere. She squatted, kneeled, and melted sideways until her whole body was on the ground. Then she put her head against the floor and laughed. George joined her there.

"This is where we live now," she said.

"I've always thought you were down-to-earth."

She could feel their messy apartment, the crumbly bits of daily life against her cheek. How was she supposed to teach their child anything if she could not even manage to use a broom? But there were other points of expertise to share. The best way to clean hair from a round brush was with a flat brush. The list of gastropods that were still alive, updated every morning at six o'clock. Not the meat loaf recipe, but the recipe for movie theater popcorn at home. You go to the movie theater, buy popcorn, bring it home. What was playing at the multiplex? Lydia was dying to see the new comedy with the actor from the lawyer show they liked, and the actress who looked like George's cousin, who was also a lawyer, but a real one. The cousin, not the actress.

Then Lydia's mind fell down a gully of pain. She was so scared that she had forgotten! They had other, urgent plans.

For once, George was scared too. When it was finally time to go, he did not swerve into traffic or make remarks, or challenge Lydia to a battle of wits. He drove them to the hospital and parked the car, carried the overnight bag, and silently helped her inside.

"I should give birth more often," she said.

While she was heavily medicated, Lydia asked George to bury her all the way down.

"What do you mean, my love?"

"Don't leave my head aboveground like some stupid folly," she slurred. "Get me in the ground good."

"Something's wrong," the doctor said.

This is what George remembered hearing. Really, the doctor did not say anything at all. Certain moments can become very literal in retrospect.

But something was wrong. The baby had the umbilical cord wrapped around her neck. A strong pair of arms shuffled George out of the room and he started crying, as if on cue. Then he was holding a paper cup of water. He thought about the funeral from all those months ago, at that horrible house, holding a mug and not remembering who had put the mug in his hands. Why was he always stranded with beverages of unknown origin? And who had died? For the life of him, he couldn't recall.

Their daughter, Anne, did not die that day; she lived. Lydia lived too. For a moment, watching Anne in her incubator, George finally understood his wife a little bit better, the way the mind tries to expand and bend itself to accommodate someone else's survival, as if such a thing were possible. Together, the couple watched the baby breathe in and out, and in again, thinking the air through her lungs. Anne fit against Lydia's chest so naturally, and Lydia fit against George. They were nested like a set of bowls. They had all outrun the shrimp, together.

George went back to work, and his graduate students presented him with a gift for his new daughter. It was a tie-dyed onesie printed with a very niche joke about Charlemagne. He knew that the pretty graduate student had picked it out. Her cheeks went red when he opened the wrapping paper, and she walked outside before everyone else, hoping he would follow.

Lydia dressed Anne in the onesie and sent a photo to George with a silly caption so he could share it with the department and thank them. She didn't quite get the Charlemagne joke but again, the Middle Ages weren't really all that funny.

"You had to be there," George often said.

"No thanks indeed!" was her reply.

After feeding, Lydia showed Anne a colorful book about a farm. No plot, just a series of animals introducing themselves, one by one. What a crock! But that is a plot, she thought, after reading the book for the seventieth time. Life as a series of introductions. Maybe there was a new edition with a series of departures. She wondered if the cows ever raced the horses in a competition for who would go extinct first. Who would be left to tend the ranch? Not the chickens, god help us. They would fly the coop. And of course, a family is an ecosystem that sometimes goes extinct too.

Anne looked up at her mother, not guessing that anything ever died. Things lived and drank milk and produced sounds. She wanted to touch the page with the fuzzy lamb, to feel the soft fibers against her skin and hear her mother make the corresponding noise.

Anne had dozens of picture books, but there was one that Lydia and George read to her every night. Most of the details have been lost. It went something like this.

There was once a king, and a kingdom, and an old, crumbling tower, a folly on the edge of the royal grounds. After letting it sit empty for a while, the king hired a man to live in the ruins and work as his hermit. The hermit dressed in a yellowed tunic, a cap, and a cape, and he was conscripted to listen to travelers and their woes. Seeing as the hermit was just a regular man with a debt to the king, he did not have any specific wisdom to impart. And so, he invented a sham, a game to satisfy the passersby, and to entertain himself.

"If you walk around the tower two times backward, you can choose one of two fates," he would say. The first fate was to live forever. The second fate was to die alone.

Of course, both fates were the very same. But the hermit's visitors seemed satisfied with the riddle. They tromped around his home, stumbling in reverse, and then of course they chose to live forever. They left his domain feeling like they knew something about the future and how to greet it. They were less afraid.

The hermit's game became very popular in the village and beyond. He set up a small souvenir shop nearby, with key chains and bumper stickers, mugs that declared this kingdom was, in fact, for lovers.

Finally, the king visited his hermit. He had heard good reviews and wanted to see for himself. The hermit read him the possible fates: live forever, die alone. And the king laughed. He was a kind king but not an idiot.

"That's just two ways of saying the same thing!" the king said. "Give me a real bit of wisdom."

"You want real wisdom? Hire a real wise guy," the hermit said. "I'm just some doof who owes you money."

"But haven't you learned anything out here all alone in the woods? Hasn't wisdom come to meet you?" the king asked.

"I have learned that no one lives forever, and that if you don't want to die alone, you should keep better tabs on the queen. Catch my meaning?"

After that, the king banished his hermit and hired a new one. A professional.

No, it wasn't a book for children. It was something else. It was a word problem, or an article on feudal states. It was maybe from a eulogy.

NOTHING WENT WRONG, but nothing went right. People came to meet the baby, and then no one came for a very long time. Lydia often missed George from the other room. She could always call for him, but yelling seemed unnecessary, and loud. George longed for solitude but was afraid. What if he never liked his own company quite as much as Lydia did? Ah, loneliness, they thought to themselves. The kind that walks around in pairs.

"Who's that guy?" Lydia said. She hadn't caught the first ten minutes of the movie.

"Who is anyone, really," George said, cradling a handful of popcorn.

The two anonymous characters drove around in circles, and Lydia never learned their names or what they meant to each other.

Sometimes Anne cried at a volume tuned to shatter their loneliness, and then their loneliness reassembled itself in a series of abrupt, awkward sketches. Lydia en-

tered the bedroom looking for George, right when he had
left the apartment to look for Lydia. They sat across from
each other in silence, then started speaking at the same
time.

"No, you," George said.

"But you," Lydia said.

Lydia made a pun about recycling that was not worth
repeating. She checked for a stray cane coming around
a corner to drag her offstage. After all, it was what she
deserved.

George made a grilled cheese sandwich and added the
butter to the pan after the bread was already hot. He had
not yet grated the cheddar.

"Oh, interesting. Is that how you're going to do it?"
Lydia asked, peering over his shoulder.

Their home was too big when they desired each other
and too small when they were fighting. It was never the
right size. It was wrong in both directions. They argued
about why they were arguing, until every argument collapsed on itself and fit precariously in the bad kitchen cabinet where the miscellany of their marriage languished in
obscurity. The heavy jar of coins, the tower of sponges, the
ruined Tupperwares turned permanently red with sauce.
None of the dishes matched, and Lydia's set of elegant
glassware was missing a piece. She put Anne down on her
activity mat and wound the toy that hopped on one foot.
Lydia wondered if this loneliness, gone unmanaged, would
become a member of their marriage, would become the

thing that in fact made their marriage possible. So invasive that if ever properly treated, it would have to end in death.

When Anne was two years old, they attended another funeral, this time in a normal room across town. She had been an esteemed colleague in the history department. Lydia had met her several times, with George, at faculty gatherings. The professor had always seemed breathless and flushed, which Lydia had loved. Now she thought maybe it had been a sign of underlying illness.

"Come on, Anne. Where there's death, there's bagels," George said, buckling his daughter into the car seat and kissing her nose.

"Jesus, don't say things like that," Lydia said. "It's a tragedy."

"She was sick for a long time," George said, not turning around. "And anyway, she wasn't your friend. She was mine."

Anne gurgled. "Dad!"

This is how their conversations had been going lately, blind alleys and impasses where there had once been an endless volley of words. Lydia used to think they would never run out of things to talk about. But most resources run out, so why then not conversation? Extinction knows no bounds. Pretty soon she would be writing an essay about the death of dialogue. A crisis for cafés across the world. She piled her curls on top of her head and shook them down around her shoulders, the way George used to like. Her style was cut shorter now, and the effect was less dramatic, but maybe the action would soften him. Or maybe if he didn't like it, he would at least remember that he used to like it and find the memory of liking it just as nice.

"Do you need a hair thing?" he asked, handing Anne her bun-bun.

"No, never mind. Let's get on the road."

The funeral was beautiful. Laughter and good food and people hugging other people with no space between their bodies. This was a person who was loved and respected. The word *treasured* hovered over the proceedings. George gave some brief remarks during the service about how his colleague had championed him early in his career, how she had gone to the mat for him when no one else had believed in his potential.

I believed in you, Lydia thought, sitting in the crowd, though she knew that was not what he had meant. She was feeling uncharitable more and more, and doing this horrible thing, looking for ways that his words could hurt her, seeking out the obsolete meaning resting dormant in whatever he chose to say. She was trying to foreshadow their underlying illness, just in case she had to look back for proof.

George took his seat next to her. Then a very pretty graduate student spoke about how there were so few opportunities for women in this field, but this woman had been a mentor to all, had made anything seem possible. The whole time she spoke, she was looking at George.

"Is that one of yours?" Lydia asked.

It was a neutral question, George thought, but his wife was always asking neutral questions that contained hidden traps. He pretended not to hear her.

"Did you hear me?"

"Yes," he said.

After the remarks were made, Lydia found herself at the refreshments table. She vaguely remembered that odd, uncomfortable funeral from a few years back. The monogrammed ladle and the etched crystal punch bowl. What was in that punch? Who had died, again?

An older man joined her, and she poured him a drink, then one for herself. She recognized him as the husband of the deceased professor. He was very handsome, with bright curious eyes and a bald head like a smooth and gorgeous planet.

"Oh, I'm so sorry for your loss," Lydia said. Anne was sitting on her hip and stole his attention.

"Mine now," she said, touching his sleeve.

"How old?" he asked with a smile.

"About two, but who's counting. I feel like I'm carrying a freight train."

"I'll bet. My eldest is twenty-four."

"And what kind of freight train is she?" Lydia asked.

"Oh, mostly import-export. Here she is now," the professor's husband said, ushering over the pretty graduate student.

"Hi, I'm Patricia," the girl said. "I've heard so much about you." Her face was covered in freckles and her hair was tucked behind her ears in two neat columns. She was even prettier up close. "I'm in your husband's group."

Lydia thought how odd it was, the way Patricia had talked about her mother during the funeral. A few weeks later, she ran into the older man at the grocery store, and after they recognized each other, then discussed the coupon flyer, and climates, both political and environmental, she could not help but bring it up. She was always saying exactly the wrong thing, tucking her foot directly under her tongue, letting every petty thought make its way toward language.

"Patricia, you know, she kept calling her mother a mentor, not her mother," Lydia said, passing a can of tomatoes back and forth between her hands.

"Why should that be odd?" the man said. "She was a mentor too."

"Okay," Lydia said.

"Mentor!" Anne said from the front seat of the shopping cart. She grabbed at the bags of wild rice. "Mentors."

"I'm glad that my daughter's role models are at least high in fiber."

"See?" he said, laughing. "Don't complicate things."

He said the same thing two weeks later, when they crossed paths at a lecture in a small bookstore and she tried to expound on the themes of the talk. Of course, she had been only half listening. Lydia was a champion daydreamer.

"Oh, and that one comment toward the end," she said. "The part about really listening."

"It was a bore," he said. "Don't complicate things." He gave her his phone number printed on an old-fashioned calling card.

"We should have food together," he said. "You look so sad."

"No, you're the one who's supposed to be sad!"

Before she could tell if he was hurt by such a stupid remark, he laughed and walked off to greet some old friends. She wondered how he and his wife had greeted people together, when they were a couple. Did she do the schmoozing, or did he? Or was it a duet?

"A duet," he said when eventually she asked him. "I am still sometimes waiting for her to chime in with the second verse. It's silly. I will probably wait for the rest of my life."

They had lunch every Thursday at a café while Anne was at her play group. They mostly talked about the news, and television programs, and sometimes about Lydia's articles. He was a professor in the English department.

"Ah," she said, "so you also specialize in extinction."

Lydia drank espresso and the professor had tea and a croissant, and a very grumpy waiter tried to get them to order an actual, honest-to-god meal.

"Have a salad," the waiter said. "It won't kill you."

"That's exactly what they say right before they feed you lethal salad," Lydia said.

Sometimes, after lunch, they would walk to the park and continue talking around whatever topic pleased them. They passed an oncoming brigade of ducks and made their way to a pond at the center of the meadow. Or they stopped at the benches near the edge of the path and watched a cavalcade of bikes ascend the steep hill. The professor had wonderful, impatient hands, which he devoted to the articulation of difficult ideas. She hoped to one day be the subject of his enthusiasm. On a certain afternoon, he bemoaned the final chapter in a disappointing book: "A torrent of vituperation!" Did people really say these things? Lydia nodded, but agreement was not the same as affection. And yet, she could not bear to sacrifice agreement, when it was all she had! Lydia was not familiar with the disappointing book in question. She was busy concocting a daydream where George died heroically, painlessly. A funeral procession of ducks and bikes. She had to knock off her husband before she could properly fantasize about anyone, it was only fair. But there she was again, thinking people dead, and worrying her head would make it so.

If Lydia ever brought anyone back to life, it was the professor's wife, so she could feel jealous without feeling macabre. They would meet for dessert like adults. Here, have an éclair, don't mind me.

Winter, spring, and summer all passed, and on their regular walks and lunches, Lydia learned her new friend's seasonal attributes. The donning and shedding of scarves, hands both gloved and bare, a chapped row of knuckles soon smooth with a slight change in weather. The loafers without socks and the boots with rings of striped wool peeking out from their tops. Something nudged at Lydia's heart, imagining how the garments had arrived in the old professor's life, if his wife had furnished his closet for the eventuality of her death, or if his daughter and sons gave him sweaters for the holidays. Or maybe he wandered through department stores with his impeccable taste, browsing the random Oxford collars and blazers, drifting from one aisle to the next, alone.

She asked if he wanted to go shopping with her, and he gave Lydia his stern professor face, as if she were an outrageous person, a ridiculous event without precedent.

"I just thought you might like an unbiased opinion," Lydia said.

"Do I look so very terrible to you?" he asked.

"No, the opposite. In fact, maybe you could give me some pointers."

He laughed. He was wearing a perfectly tailored shirt, and she wished she could touch his perfect sleeve for no reason, the way Anne would. Mine, Lydia thought. Possessions always made Lydia so sad, and she had never been sure why. Now she knew, yes, it's because they stay here forever. Possessions are the loneliest things in the world, lonelier even than people, because we leave them all behind. When everything finally went extinct, the planet would be a walk-in closet, with no one around to brag about having a walk-in closet.

One day, the café was closed. There was a note on the door. The grumpy waiter, whose name was Simon, was getting married to the chef's daughter, Sylvia. The whole restaurant staff was at City Hall. They peered in the darkened window and saw tables arranged in long rows with gauzy napkins and pretty centerpieces.

The professor invited Lydia to eat at his place instead.

"Would that be fine with your wife?" she asked.

"What she doesn't know can't kill her. Because she's dead."

Pass the scones, nothing to see here.

Lydia said yes. "But only because Simon wouldn't want us to skip lunch."

They walked upstairs and he unlocked the door, and they left their shoes in the hall. Lydia joined him in the kitchen to help fetch seltzers from the fridge.

He made them chicken salad on pumpernickel, and they ate sitting next to each other on the low, deep couch. On the coffee table, he placed a small plate of sour pickles, a bowl of gymnastically folded potato chips, and for dessert, a round glass dish with ice-cold strawberries. His home was cozy and smelled good, and had the feeling of stuff without the feeling of clutter. Every vase was a gift from someone special and every book was dog-eared. He had put a shelf on the radiator and on the shelf were old photographs of his kids, his friends, people he loved. Just being in the apartment made Lydia feel like something with a really charming backstory.

"What is this?" she asked, pointing to a delicate green leaf sprouting from the sandwich.

"That's watercress."

"I like it. I like watercress."

"I like you," he said. "Thank you for keeping me company."

He was really kind to her. It felt as if no one had liked her in one hundred years.

He moved the sandwich off her lap and put his hand on her leg. She was so hungry for him then that it was overwhelming, like humidity descending on the entire city.

"What?" he asked.

"Nothing," she said, taking his hand in hers.

"Well?" he said.

Lydia climbed into his arms and they undressed right there. When they embraced she could feel him shivering all over.

"Well!" she said.

He moved their plates and seltzers to the floor so they wouldn't get knocked about. Lydia was on top of him now, and she reached to close the ugly blinds, which she worried was presumptuous, both finding them ugly and closing them, since this was not her home.

The room was very dark. She had never seen him before, in shadow. There was so much she didn't know. For instance, had a doctor checked that mole, or was it watercress?

The next part was so earnest it made them laugh, which led to a more serious approach, the way laughter often does when people aren't wearing clothes. Her breathing became heavy and desperate, and they laughed again at the incredibly serious turn things had taken, which only made the moment even more dire.

"May I?" he asked.

And then he did!

Later, she curled against him and cried.

"Why tears?" he asked.

"I shouldn't have done that."

"It's all right. It's fine."

"Is it fine?"

"Don't complicate things," he said, and he smoothed her hair down along her neck.

"I shouldn't have done this," she said, and a few minutes later they did it again. They did it a few weeks after that, and then another time in winter. It was so cold, what did they expect?

"Never again," she said after the last time. Then she cried, because she knew she had to put an end to it and would not see him anymore. He was gentle and good. He was a good person who would be all alone. Or was it that she would be all alone? Lydia hoped her math was wrong and that he would live forever. She was always shitty with numbers. She wanted everyone she loved to survive her, but also, she wanted to never die.

"I don't know why I tried to be your friend in the first place," she said. "I'm so selfish."

"Most friendship is feigning," he said, "most loving really foolish."

She cried even harder then, because she was curled against a man who could not even properly quote Shakespeare. She grabbed her clothing and dressed as quickly as possible.

Pulling up her pants, Lydia found a small card in one of the pockets, folded into an accordion shape. *Please join us for refreshments and remembrances.*

WE SHOULD PROBABLY check and see if the king was ever able to keep tabs on the queen.

When the professional hermit took over, the queen started visiting him at night, just as she had visited the hermit before him. The king banished this new hermit and replaced him with another, then another, and one more. The queen conquered them all.

"What can I tell you? I have a type," she said.

She could not resist draping their capes over her body afterward, the way the rough fabric felt against her skin in the moonlight. She loved running through the forest with nothing but the sound of insects at her feet.

The king was exhausted. He loved the queen so much. She loved him too. But people in villages talk, and their kingdom was at stake.

His advisers begged him to consider finding a side piece of his own. They brought a series of townspeople to his bedchamber, each one more beautiful and handsome and doting than the last. There was this one stonemason with a particular way about him. But you can't solve a problem by doubling it. And he didn't want to do something just because the queen did! The king was kind of punk rock.

Instead, he went to the palace horticulturalist for a remedy or a potion, and she applied dandelions in embarrassing places.

"Are you sure this will work?" he asked, adjusting his pants.

"Trust me!" the horticulturalist said, stuffing some clover in each of his pockets and pinching his tush.

Next, the king stopped over to see the castle librarian. In a different kind of fable, he would've fallen in love with her mild-mannered temperament and mysterious past. But when he asked for a recommendation, she always suggested Chaucer. Chaucer this, Chaucer that! After a while he was convinced she had never read anything else.

"Shh," the librarian said, lowering her gaze. Her cheek paled. Was she sexy, or was it plague?

Finally, the king visited his cranky royal astronomer in the north tower.

"Don't touch my cosmos!" the astronomer yelled, apoplectic, rearranging the orrery on the mantel.

"Sorry," the king said, laughing. He loved messing with the astronomer's cosmos.

"This is the Terrestrial Sphere," the astronomer said, tinkering with the heavenly orbs. "And beyond this, the Celestial Sphere. And beyond this, nothing."

"Any advice on the marital sphere?"

"Beyond this, nothing."

The king was suspicious of Aristotelian astronomy

and said as much. Then he spun the orrery without thinking.

"Whoops," the king said.

"You know, the kingdom to the south has something called a telescope," the astronomer said. "Maybe if I had a telescope, I could formulate an opinion on your dumb marriage!"

The king thought he should probably burn the royal astronomer at the stake, but stake-burnings were a real bummer. The king had a feeling that someday, with a little perspective, people would not find stake-burnings all that great.

And so he left the north tower and traveled across several mountains to find the original hermit he had banished. The hermit was now a butcher, with four children and a house that was not crumbling, nor was it a sham. His apron said WORLD'S BEST DAD. All the magic in his life was real.

"Have you heard the one about Charlemagne?" the kids asked the king, and then they ran off to play.

The butcher poured them some drinks and they traded stories.

"You're the only one who has ever given me any true wisdom," the king confessed, his head in his hands. He brought the butcher up to speed and asked him for advice. A baby crawled over the butcher's shoulders, and he packed him in a blanket like he was making a sandwich, put his son to sleep in the glow of the fire.

"The answer is clear," the butcher said. He sent the

king on his way with a solution and a rack of ribs coated in a secret family spice blend.

Of course, why not ask the queen if she herself wanted to be the hermit?

She jumped up and wrapped her arms around the king's neck and moved to the woods that very night. They were happy. Every evening, the king came to visit her, and she met him in the moonlight, covered them both in the wool cape.

WHEN PATRICIA TOLD George about her father and his wife, together, he was surprised. He was a little bit angry too.

"But why?" she said, tucking her hair behind her ears, pulling the sheets up around her chest. "If us, why not them?"

That was true. But the word *us* really made him cringe. George and his wife had used to be an us, and somehow, the word had changed meaning when he hadn't been paying attention. He did not know words could do that, swap their key components overnight. George reached over Patricia to grab his phone from the pillow. There were no messages from Lydia, no worried missives, no one frantic to find out if he was dead or alive or something in between. The last note sent between them was from days before, a question asked across the rooms of their apartment. He had thumbed the letters with one hand instead of traversing the short, easy space between them. A longing emerged at the bottom of George's stomach, for the time when someone was afraid of losing him. That's how he knew he had already been lost.

He sat with the feeling for a while and Patricia moved around her room naked. She stacked her papers on her desk and placed an article that George had mentioned on her nightstand, so he would know that she was reading it too. She brought him a glass of water from the sink and plugged in his phone. She could tell that he was feeling unloved, so she populated the room with her feelings, hoping they would become his. Maybe in the morning he would see. Then she put on his T-shirt and went to sleep.

Eventually, George got up the nerve to confront his wife. He knew that Lydia could not resist a competition, so he suggested that this would be the best way to approach their separation.

"I don't understand. What kind of contest is divorce?" she asked, holding Anne in her lap on the floor.

"An adult contest."

"Oh, is that what you call leaving your family?"

"Maybe I'll lose. Maybe I'll come back."

"Maybe we won't be here, and you'll have to eat crow."

"Look, you know the crows have been gone for years," he said. "And anyway, that would count as a forfeit."

"What about Anne?" she asked.

"I'll see her all the time." George picked his daugh-

ter up off the ground and swung her around until she
squealed.

"Funny Daddy," Lydia said, not laughing. What was
the punch line? That he hadn't dropped her?

"Funny Mommy," he said, putting Anne back into her
arms.

"Already you're keeping a tally?" she asked.

"That one was a practice round."

THE SEPARATION WAS a long contest with no rules and no
scoreboard. It lasted most of Anne's early childhood. Her
parents called it the relay sometimes when they were dropping her off or picking her up. Other times they called it
the competition, the homecoming game, the sprint. Anne
liked games. She liked the one where you run in a circle
until everyone falls over. She liked duck, duck, possum
(the geese were gone). She didn't like winning, she liked
playing.

"Mommy, I like the feeling of everyone on the ground
laughing," she said. It was her fifth birthday party, and
everyone was on the ground laughing, even Grandma
Rose. Her grandma's knees were muddy, and she scooped
Anne into her lap, and they all stayed there for a while,
just talking and playing. Her grandma asked Anne to
sing the song with the made-up words ("All songs have
made-up words, Grandma Rose!") and to bring the plastic
clamshell of frosted cupcakes over from the picnic table.

Anne got to have two birthday parties every year, and she liked them both the same. This was what she told people, and she said it so often that it became true. She did not spend a lot of time back then thinking about different degrees of love. Love, as she knew it, always arrived in equal amounts.

When Anne turned six, her dad had a brief illness. She wasn't supposed to tell her mom about it, but her mom found out anyway. Her mom was good at finding things. Lydia drove to George's apartment and brought him a box of knickknacks and some strange bumper stickers, and left them outside his door. Anne asked if she could play with the old magnet in the box, with the mug that was for lovers, but her dad said no. Her mom said he was not always such a strict person, but for a lot of reasons he was now very strict and stern and that was okay too, that was a kind of love. He was always worried about Anne's leaning too far out the windows, even though the windows had bars. When she was seven, he still made her hold his hand crossing the street. Even Patricia let her cross the street alone, in front of an adult, so long as she looked both ways.

When George was sick, Lydia brought him dinner if he would allow it. She was furious that he hadn't told her sooner, but that was when she thought things were more serious.

"My degree is terminal. My illness is not," he said.

"You're such an idiot," she said, crying. "Where's Patricia?"

"I broke up with her. A month ago."

"Oh, you really are an idiot. I had no idea I procreated with such a dummy!"

"I didn't have a choice."

"You should've married that girl. Her hair was perfect."

"You can't get married when you aren't divorced," he said, coughing. He walked across the room to get a drink.

Lydia didn't say anything to that. It was true, they had never gotten around to filing the paperwork. It was too expensive anyway to declare a marriage extinct. When an animal goes extinct, the paperwork is free.

"Why didn't you ask me? I would've done it." She was trying to be considerate, but the words wounded him all the same. He looked so thin in his Middle Ages. She looked around his apartment and did not recognize the brand of soap he used, the squished loaf of nutty bread he bought. The daily decisions they used to make together had diverged. George was wearing a sweater she did not remember, some gray situation with buttons and a little pocket. She hated the sweater. No. She was jealous of it.

"Maybe we shouldn't meet like this anymore," George said, buffing the wood table with the edge of his thumb.

"Oh."

"Well, I can't imagine that what's-his-name likes you coming over here all the time."

"There is no what's-his-name."

"The one from the magazine?" George asked.

"Honey, magazines haven't existed in years."

They laughed together at that, but still, it was the last time she came over for dinner.

Before the publication folded, Lydia had written an article about the extinction of extinction. That was really the nail in the coffin, her editor said.

Now she was working on a book about certain types of flora and fauna that survive, despite inhospitable realities. The book was called *In Ruins* and it had a photorealistic painting of a crumbling edifice on the cover. It's out of print, but you can still find it if you know where to look.

THE QUEEN LIVED happily for many years as a hermit. The king still came to visit her every night, and they took each other in every position, some bad, some good, out in the forest, beneath the stars, and afterward always collapsing in a heap on her cot. Sometimes they stayed awake like little nocturnal beasts, talking away the darkness, then berries for breakfast and more aerobic lovemaking under the dawn firmament, during the brief hour when the sun and the moon stood in the sky together.

One day, he didn't show. She waited for him, but it was soon morning, afternoon, evening again, the light changing with her worry. No word from the king. She hung the CLOSED sign on the folly and walked through the woods, over the drawbridge, and back to the castle, where burial and funeral arrangements were already underway.

His body was on display for visitors in the throne

room. They had dressed him in the awful shirt that pinched around his neck. The king looked so much older than he had looked the other day. What age are you when you are dead? The queen touched his hand. She did not know.

"I'm still your queen," she said to the attendants, with a haughty affect she had not used in years.

"We weren't sure," they replied, "if you were."

"Fair," she said.

The palace librarian caught up with her in the great hall.

"I think this will really help," she said, and handed her a copy of *The Canterbury Tales*.

The queen went to her old keep, the rooms covered in bedsheets, and slumped on the pink divan that had been a gift from a rude duke. She ordered in food every night and when it arrived, lost her appetite. She cleaned out the armoire, threw away old tchotchkes, traced the patterns on her heirloom tapestries. Constellations, galaxies, predicted by royal astronomers, then carefully sewn and preserved in the sanctum of the castle. Earth, the center of the universe! What a relief.

The king kissed the queen on her bare shoulder, and she could feel his lips lingering there even after her eyes opened. She missed him so much that sometimes, in the moments before waking, he was still alive.

"Enough," she said. She stole a tapestry or two and went home.

Back to the folly, back to the chorus of insects, back

to the clouds that could only be observed between the necks of trees. The smell of pine and mulch filled her with endless comfort. Even the rotting berry bush smelled good. She tied the cape around her neck and let it cascade along her body, but one of the folds remained creased. And so the queen gathered the fabric in her hands and shook, then shook again, and shook once more. The cape billowed at its seams until a young woman emerged from the cloth. She'd been hiding there, like a toddler tucked behind a curtain.

"Are you a child?" the queen asked.

"I'm your child," the young woman said.

"That's strange," the queen said. "How long have you been here?"

"Oh, the normal amount of time," her daughter said. She was probably the same age the queen had been when she'd married the king.

"Would you like to tell me what I've missed?" the queen asked. But she was no longer a queen. She was a hermit again, and also (even though she couldn't name it) a mother.

She listened to the girl's tale, which was really just a series of introductions. There was a long tangent about her friends, her lovers, and something called an internship. The sky darkened and the evening animals emerged, braying and howling in the forest. How odd the world felt at night, lodged between what had happened, and whatever happened next. The girl reported a series of plans that would have sounded to anyone like a very good life indeed. But whether she got to live them, or just describe them, no one can really say.

WHEN ANNE TURNED seven, she learned to ride a bicycle. When she turned eight, the English professor died in his sleep. Her mother sat at the kitchen counter and cried on the phone. It was a stroke, unexpected. Anne knew the expression "a stroke of luck" from a chapter book she was reading, but that didn't sound quite right in this context. She pictured a brushstroke from her watercolor set looping over his dreaming eyes, painting L-U-C-K in cursive.

"It's a different kind of thing," her mom said. "Sometimes words are tricky like that."

At the funeral, Lydia went over to say hello to Patricia, who had married a very successful athlete. Anne dove into Patricia's arms.

"Thank you for coming," the pretty grad student said. She wasn't a grad student anymore. She still had freckles, and also faint creases around her eyes. She was beautiful. Lydia had spent so much time wondering about her over the years. What was that mauve lipstick she wore? How did she always smell like she had just gone for a swim? All she could think now was that Patricia had no parents.

"To be honest, I wasn't sure if you would want me here," Lydia said.

"Of course I do," Patricia said, putting a hand on her

shoulder. "You're family. Excuse me," she said, and went to look after her other guests. As she walked across the room, Lydia saw George standing against a wall, waiting to say hello. He was holding a shared party plate out to her. A bagel, a deli salad, a pile of fruit. She remembered how, at their wedding, he had brought them a saucer full of limes with two spoons. They had been so busy dancing that they had forgotten to eat.

"But, Dad, melon is not my favorite," Anne said, grabbing a slice from the plate, and they both smiled.

AFTER THAT, THEY started taking long drives together. Sometimes they would have a destination in mind. A museum, or a park that Anne would especially like. Lydia would push her on the swings and George would catch her at the bottom of the slide, or encourage her from the top of the slide, or lift her off the middle of the slide into his arms when she did not want to scoot all the way down. Sometimes the drive was the point of things, and they would get lost in a town out of state. They went on a hike and arrived at a scenic lookout, where a soft campfire smell drifted up and over Anne's face. It was her first time in the woods.

One hot day in autumn, they spotted a beautiful old home off the shoulder of the road.

"Look," Lydia said.

"A castle!" Anne cried.

"A house," George said.

He took the next exit and they drove for a mile or

two before ending up in front of a long, snaking driveway. One of those paved entrances that could have been
a moat in another era. But the house was just a normal
house. A split-level with pretty window boxes and a lush,
green lawn. At the end of the ridiculous driveway hung a
Realtor's sign: FOR SALE.

"Where are we?" Lydia asked, looking around.

"You have reached your destination!" Anne said.

Lydia squeezed Anne's hands from over the back of
her seat. "But when are we?" she asked.

"Half past four," George said.

"So late!" Lydia said. "It's nearly five."

"That's just two ways of saying the same thing," George
said. They unbuckled their seat belts and climbed out of
the car.

The azalea bushes were still in full bloom even though
it was late in the season. The front door was unlocked.
Hadn't they done this before?

"Hello," Lydia called before entering. When no one answered, they walked through the empty rooms. One wall
looked perfect for hanging family photos, Lydia thought.
She could picture a dresser here, an end table there. Chenille and linen, like from a catalog.

"Check this out," George said. He somehow knew
where to find the side entrance, and opened it to reveal
the trees, gardens, endless exploring.

"I think this is right on the edge of the nature preserve," he said, looking at his phone. "It would take a year
to walk all the trails."

Anne ran under his arm and out into the meadow, where a crumbling structure caught her eye. She fell and skinned her knee in the grass but rallied and kept running, until she reached the domed shade of the princess's lair. Everything looked out of a fairy tale. She put her new toy with the braided lanyard on top of a high rock and called to her parents.

"What is that? Is that safe?" Lydia asked, pointing to their daughter.

"It's a folly," George said.

"What's the purpose?" Lydia said.

"It's decorative. It doesn't have a purpose."

"Ah, another extinction to add to my list."

"If it never had a reason, can it ever go extinct?" George asked.

"That's actually the title of my next book," Lydia said, laughing. She wanted to smooth the sleeve of his jacket but wasn't sure if that was okay. Don't complicate things, she thought, and reached for him.

"Run to me!" Anne was yelling in the distance.

The couple looked at each other.

"Shall we?" George asked.

"It's your funeral," Lydia said. She could not resist a contest. Anne would be the referee and decide who had won. Lydia tightened her laces, and George stretched his legs. Then they ran as fast as they could, without stopping.

Anne watched her parents fumbling toward her. They looked absurd, and also, amazing. It wasn't until later, after they bought the house and moved in, long after, that she would understand their limitations. Of course, they died, but the order of things doesn't matter. This is one of the last good days that Anne remembers, and if memory is what we have left, when all is said and done, it may as well have happened at the very end.

FORTRESS

STEPHANIE DOES NOT REMEMBER THE FIRST TIME SHE MADE space. She was an infant in her crib, mesmerized by a mobile sewn of felted stars and moons. One night, without explanation, the ceiling rose an extra foot, and the mobile detached from its hook, landing on the baby like a mechanical claw around a toy. Luckily no one was harmed. Each of her parents blamed the incident on the other, not noticing or questioning the new expanse of air that soared above their heads. The mobile—reattached ("Did we need a ladder last time?"), then stuffed in a drawer ("Why did we hang this so high?"), then sold at a garage sale. Before long, Stephanie was a toddler, conscious of how she could warp a room to fit her desire. Come, she had been saying, before she could speak. Come hold me. I'll make my nursery larger so you can find me here.

THEN AGAIN—MOST BEGINNINGS, apocryphal. Almost always unobserved. Who can remember with any accuracy life's initial drift toward its final shape? Before the incident in the crib. Earlier, her mother's belly. Nothing horrible, just a surge of space hidden in an already expanding pattern. Whirling around the womb with inches to spare.

THE BABYSITTER WATCHED Stephanie disappear behind the couch. A game of hide-and-seek, but it went on too long. She peered under the cushions and there was nothing, just coins entombed in clouds of dust. Then the panic, the search across every inch of the property. The cupboard, the attic, the backyard. The woods at the end of the block. The babysitter looked toward the trees, holding the phone, trying to decide if this was an emergency. Hard to know until you've had one.

Stephanie, under the floorboards, a new and secret place. Cool, calm, safe. She lifted the planks when she was tired, rolled out from beneath the sofa, and grabbed the babysitter's hand.

"Tuck me in," she said.

The teenager sobbed and hugged her.

"Oh, thank god, thank god. I would have been dead meat."

"Tell me a story," Stephanie said. "We can be dead meat together."

The babysitter read the book Stephanie loved, about visiting the nice doctor. An appointment where the patient gets bad news. Was this the same book from last time?

"I don't want to scare you," the nice doctor said.

Then they played with the blocks that were always slightly bigger than the babysitter remembered.

STEPHANIE'S LITTLE SISTER, a bundle in the crook of Mom's arm. The house, smaller for the first time. Close and nice and the smell of waffles. Dad glued glow-in-the-dark stars on their ceiling, and at night Stephanie could make them spread across the room into constellations. Her little sister laughed. Their cat curled on a ledge with its tail cavorting in midair. Its spot in the sun, so much wider after spending time in Stephanie's mind.

Sandboxes could get larger. Ball pits could get deeper. The neighbor's doghouse could get taller. Hopscotch forever, an endless array of squares, hopping on sore feet until there was nowhere else to go but back to the beginning. Stephanie thought about hand-me-downs, how her sister was growing every day. A leg, an arm, now fitting through a flannel sleeve, a corduroy pant, into a place where Stephanie had already been. In that way, they had the same magic. Growing to meet each other somewhere good.

On the playground, her little sister always ran to the edge of the grass, where the street bent into traffic. Their mother wore sunglasses all day long. She wore them sitting on the bench in the park, drinking from an opaque cup.

"Why do you wear those inside and outside?" Stephanie asked, tugging at her mother's leg.

"They're prescription," she said.

"Prescription for what?"

"Depression. Go play."

When Stephanie's little sister ran to the edge of the grass, Stephanie would make the playground larger, but only by a few inches each time. She knew she was doing something wrong, but the reasons were not clear. Adult rules eluded her. Eventually the town parks committee investigated a zoning violation, dispatching a crew of landscape artists and then scientists from the community college to take stock of the Sycamore Recreation Center and its dangerous adjacent intersection. But that was much later. By then, Stephanie had already outgrown the playground, had learned how to leave a place the way she'd found it.

One afternoon her little sister ran too fast toward the street, and Stephanie could not make the grass stretch to meet her.

A horrible thump, the type of sound that cannot be digested. Then the smell of burnt rubber.

The playground had a jungle gym, a slide, a seesaw, and an array of dandelions that faded into the curb. It was a really good playground, but it was closed for a whole year.

At the funeral, Stephanie focused her energy on expanding the size of the grave. She imagined the small coffin traveling deeper and deeper into the ground, traveling all the way through to the other side, where her sister would emerge from the soil and live the rest of her life very far away. They could both continue living as long as they were on opposite ends of the earth, Stephanie decided, like a kind of gravity that holds love in orbit.

HER PARENTS FOUND a way to create distance all by themselves. A different kind of distance. Not like Stephanie's enchanted spaces. Each person marooned in a separate part of the house. Stranded, like Robinson Crusoe. Stephanie imagined herself on an island in the middle of the Aegean Sea. A place on a map that had borders and boundaries and shores. Longitude. Latitude. Easy to find, finger to globe, you are here. Stephanie worried that she would never be easy to find. Always changing the street signs, always lost. Finger to globe, where are you now? She finished her sister's old coloring books. After she had colored inside the lines, she went back and colored outside the lines too.

COME, SHE WAS saying in her sleep. Come find me here. That was the night she made the whole house larger by a quarter mile.

At first, her mother only noticed the wallpaper, divided into mismatched sections where the pattern used to rendezvous in neat strips.

"Hey, look at this," she said, turning away from the television for the first time in days, touching the doors, their hinges popping. It was the exact sound her best friend in elementary school used to make, cracking her knuckles before tossing a ball; it sounded just like that, but better. Someone had adjusted the volume, tuned the memory to its most ideal coordinates. "Look," she said once more, and the moldings splayed. But Stephanie's father couldn't hear her. He was downstairs in the den, watching the room widen around the sleeper sofa into a different kind of room, one that nevertheless felt familiar.

Then the floorboards, warped and wavering, curving with the strain. Her parents wandered the house in amazement, a wonder that dissolved into something frantic, their feet reaching the end of a hallway only to have it stretch out and away. Recognition met them at each corner, but a recognition mixed with terror. The feeling of remembering something that had been purposely forgotten. The feeling of forgetting something that had not yet happened.

"Where are you?" Stephanie's father said. Where was he? He was stumbling in circles, then later, screaming—but not yet. It was as if he knew he would be screaming shortly and felt that it could wait. When he looked at the windows, he could see what happened next, even if he wasn't sure why. Stephanie's mother, lifting her leg for the bottom stair, watching the floor disappear beneath her heel, tumbling to a carpet that belonged in her youngest daughter's room, stowed away. But no, it was here. How? She couldn't bear it, the daisy pattern woven around its edge.

"Honey?" she asked, but there was no response. She wasn't sure if honey was Stephanie, or her husband, or a buried version of herself.

The screaming finally started when the windows shifted in their frames. Shattered like sheets of brittle candy on a pan. Her father supposed the house would not quit until it broke to bits. He could see himself, moments ahead, helping it along. And so, he did. He took a chair—the closest object—and smashed it through a wall, hoping to quake loose the spell.

Awake then, cold and sweaty, Stephanie gripped the edges of her bed, the thin mattress pancaked in her fists. The house stopped expanding, and her parents found themselves in the kitchen, clutched each other there. Absolute silence. It was the first time they had touched in months. The drawers were all distended from their sleeves. Refrigerator magnets, scattered across the tile. Her mother vomited on the floor, right where the cat used to cough up hairballs. Where was the cat?

At first, the mind attaches a haunting to a ghost, and so of course they thought of their daughter who was gone. It must have been her, their baby returning, the house expanding to bring her home. But then they remembered—they did not believe in ghosts. They remembered other things too. Clues, evidence of something they had not been able to explain, and so they had not bothered to try. The mind corrects for inconsistencies so that living can continue.

The moon-and-stars mobile? they whispered. The too-high ceiling? The extra bit of world that hovers around our child, they thought. They never said it out loud, not precisely in so many words, but they knew it had been Stephanie. They opened her door and looked in her room, jaws tight. She had fallen back asleep.

They kept her an elbow away, over a shoulder, over the years, always in view but not close enough to hold. They were afraid of her, but they were also ashamed. Their fear had shuttled into the space between who they actually were and who they had imagined themselves to be. Until now, they had not noticed any space between these two things at all.

"I shouldn't have taken that medication when I was pregnant," Stephanie heard her mother say once, through a closed door.

"Don't be stupid," her father said. "There isn't a medication that causes this."

"That afternoon," her mother said. "Do you think she made the street wider? On purpose? The accident."

"I don't know."

"Not an accident?"

"I don't know."

Their home stayed large for a few days, but with a low, keening vibration, it gradually retracted. Settled. A house eases itself into a landscape.

Some concerned citizens filed a zoning complaint about the property, which the committee quickly dismissed. The town left them alone. Haven't those poor people been through enough? Settled.

They had lost both of their daughters, Stephanie realized, when she was older. But she felt no such sympathy for her parents in childhood. She was stranded in a borderless galaxy, like the valiant explorer who reaches the end of the universe and realizes the universe has no end.

IN MIDDLE SCHOOL, the dances, the glow sticks, the DJ pumping bass. Bubblegum-flavored lip gloss. A cute boy with a swoop of hair across his forehead, low-hanging jeans, pressed up against her from behind. She felt her skin get hot and the cafeteria expanded around her. The boy was suddenly four feet gone, dancing with a different girl, his hair hanging down over his eyes, leaving Stephanie alone in the middle of the floor. A space slightly larger than it was before. Jewel-tone lights strobing across Stephanie's cheeks, her braids, her sneakers. Stephanie running outside. The cafeteria, back to its old dimensions.

Walking home from the dance, through the Madisons' backyard, so quiet and still. She felt powerful and safe, and also like the loneliest person on earth.

A moment of confusion flickering across the cute boy's face. Was I dancing with *this* girl the whole time? Then a new song.

IN HIGH SCHOOL, tall, sad girl. Taller, taller—pinched. Standing against the brick wall in torn jeans and an over-sized shirt. That was the photo in the yearbook, any-way. Ink on the ball of her hand. Reading big books of essays, theory, poetry. She understood some but not all, hauling the hardcovers around in her messenger bag, un-der her arm. She thought that if she carried them with her, they would cross the barrier from tote to brain, would someday impart their wisdom as a way of saying thanks. But they remained opaque and large, looming in her mind for all their mystery. The paperbacks on her high shelf. Love stories, campus novels, road trips, workplace comedies, horror tales. And still, no one had written about Stephanie. Even the parts that went over her head did not consider her head, did not consider her at all. She could tell. Where was the sentence that told her what to do? Stephanie could make her lungs larger, but how to use them? She smoked cheap cigarettes near the tennis courts. So cool. Unapproachable. Alone. No witnesses—at the basketball courts—lifting a hoop aloft, stretching the radius, the braided net swinging with its newfound width.

"She walks around like a fortress," someone said at the lockers.

"How does a fortress walk?" a teacher asked, laughing. Even the faculty was in on the joke.

"I don't know. Like her. Like Stephanie."

Sometimes, Stephanie wondered if her dreams were the same size as other people's dreams. When she slept, her mind resembled the inside of a horn, or the wind caught in a turbine on a hill. Booming, spinning, yawning open. Stephanie practiced every night, harnessed her desire. She could summon small rooms inside her body where there were none, deep caverns for someone to fill, retracting them when she was through. Come find me here.

She went under the bleachers with a boy from calculus class. In the back of his car too.

"Hey, move the seat up just a bit," he said.

Then she moved the seat, but not with her hands. He

didn't notice. She could stretch his sedan into a limo if she wanted. No—he would never be able to parallel park. Just an extra inch or two for her knees, wrapped around the boy from calculus.

"I can take more of you," she said, with the shrug of someone older.

The boy blushed—did people say these things?

Stephanie had heard a woman whisper it in a bad movie, and she'd laughed, alone in the house, hysterical with relief. Finally, she could relate. But for all the wrong and impossible reasons.

Then again under the bleachers with the boy from calculus, then again in his car. There was sometimes a small dent in his right cheek. He always looked surprised, with her, and with himself. The first time she came, she was afraid she had created a new annex in his driveway. And then—the swim club in the middle of the night, the chlorine stinging her eyes. The Sycamore Recreation Center, his idea, not hers. Stephanie almost did not remember, but then of course, she did.

Finally on his futon, in his basement, the foundation of his house trembling at its borders, shaking all around them.

"Whoa," he said, launching upright. "Did you feel that?"

"Yeah, I think *you* made that happen!" Stephanie said, smiling against his nice warm face, bringing him close. He breathed deeply, taking this in. The boy from calculus on top of her, holding her tighter to his chest, desire rising inside him with nowhere to go. What must that feel like, Stephanie thought, her skin clinging to his skin. Not having a place to put the wanting, except to put it in someone else.

Walking home through the Madisons' backyard, torn jeans and still wet between her legs. What else can I make bigger? She tried to expand her mind but that never seemed to work. How to even begin. The stars are brighter in the suburbs—it was a thing people said, but Stephanie had never been anywhere else. She noticed the tree stumps along the edge of the Madisons' lawn, adapted their diameter, added rings to their concentric rings, made their lives longer in retrospect.

Teenage girl, a sudden lift of spine, looking up, pretending to want nothing. Fortress.

DOES THE CHALKBOARD get longer, or does Mr. Dougherty's handwriting get smaller? The girls snickered and Stephanie shrugged.

"Or maybe we've gotten bigger," she said. "Plumper. Fat."

The girls: horrified.

"Ew!" they said, fake retching. They shrank back into their seats; god forbid, to take up space, large spaces, any space at all.

Stephanie marveled. They were so small. If she closed one eye, they almost disappeared. She could be cruel when she wanted to be, but most of the time she didn't say a word. Every week, she traversed the sharp hexagon from locker to class to lunch to home with as few tangents as possible, the minimum surface area required to get through a day.

At the picnic tables, Stephanie stopped to look for the boy from calculus. He was with another girl, also from calculus. Their calculus class was pretty big. The girl whispered something in his ear, and he looked at her frowning, but with a grin on the other side of the expression. She drank from his water bottle. The lining of her pockets stuck out through the bottoms of her shorts, and she sat on the picnic table, throwing her head back silently and smiling into the sun. The boy from calculus leaned between her knees.

Stephanie thought, They are performing, but for whom? For each other? She watched them carefully, then walked to calculus without the boy.

He tried to meet her gaze in class, to talk to her after school.

"Hey," he said. "Hey!"

She didn't turn around. He was a familiar hangout, a local spot. Meet you at the boy from calculus! Stephanie could create places that had never existed—why would she bother visiting the same place as everyone else?

He jogged after her while she was walking home, and her desire to be alone expanded. Solitude was the only space worth having. She crossed the street. She made the sidewalk longer, but just a little. Girls her age were always running toward something, right? The pavement warped in her wake, like cement over the roots of a misbehaved tree. He could follow her forever and never catch up.

He didn't follow Stephanie forever. He watched her advance, his hands on his knees, out of breath, shaking his head. He married the Madisons' daughter, and the young couple moved in with her parents to save money. Don't even ask! he said when his friends teased him about the close quarters. But really, he loved Mr. and Mrs. Madison, Doug and Lolly, who played board games every night in the living room. His own parents had never wanted to gather in the living room, which they used for storage, stacking up boxes of soup from the Cost Cutter in town.

Eventually the boy from calculus bought the house from his in-laws, built a fence so the neighborhood kids would stop using their backyard as a shortcut. She worked in real estate, and he got involved with local politics. She listed and sold Stephanie's parents' house—"Did the previous homeowners vault this ceiling?"—but that was later. On Sundays, they barbecued shish kebab and portobello burgers in the exact spot where Stephanie had once walked at night, her head tilted back, looking at the stars. When he was very tired—a campaign for mayor, three kids—he fell asleep wedged against the headboard, just like he used to in high school. The button in the central tuft of fabric would leave a mark in the middle of his cheek.

Sometimes the boy, now a man, thought about the time he made the foundation of his house shake with lust. The memory—archived at the bottom of his modest personal mythology. He had checked the news the morning after for reports of earthquakes, tremors—no. It never happened again. It never happened with his wife, but something different happened with her. Something closer, quiet. He finally told her the story one day and she laughed—it made her love him more, this mortal fantasy of earth-rattling strength. She kissed him on the dent in his cheek. He must have known that it was Stephanie all along, his wife said. Strange girl, sad girl. Hadn't he ever considered?

No, it hadn't ever occurred to him.

Strange girl. I used to watch her out there, in the backyard. All alone.

You did?

Fortress—that's what they called her, right?

I never called her that, he said.

My sweet man. She kissed him again and again.

Playing on the edge of the lawn with his sons, he traced the rings of the tree stumps and dreamed about all the time they had left. All the time in the world.

GRADUATION, AND THE seniors tossed their caps in the air. Stephanie couldn't resist. She allowed the caps to continue rising, swelling the sky up and up. This gave the impression that the world had stopped. Her classmates talked about it for years, the way the hats just hung there on the breeze, a cluster of boys and girls in gowns, lost ghosts on the lawn, hovering and holding their breath in anticipation. Is this what the future feels like? they wondered,

marveling at the way adulthood had started without anyone's permission. Some of them swore they saw the rest
of their lives illuminated in that bright second. And then,
finally, the caps fell. Cheering. The sky restored to its
normal dimensions. Stephanie's parents caught her eye,
cowered in the bleachers. Stephanie alone, a dot on the
football field. She made her way to the parking lot, and
farther away still. If you closed one eye, she disappeared.
Away from everyone else. Barely there at all.

STEPHANIE IMAGINED HER sister finishing high school the
very same day. It was a beautiful event, with carnations
braided into necklaces that you could buy as a gift for the
graduating seniors. Her sister gave a speech—her classmates had picked her to do it, an easy choice—and afterward, everyone went to a local restaurant for cake.

STEPHANIE'S PARENTS, STUTTERING, half-hearted, offered
to drive her to college. No, she said. Marooned explorer.
Elbow's distance, arm's length, waving goodbye. A scholarship too. She touched the spot where her father had
slammed a chair through the wall, all those years ago.
Never fixed. Buckled her purse. She packed two suitcases
and went to school alone.

A taxi to the train. A pop song playing through a tinny
speaker. Her parents: smaller in the rearview mirror, but
that was physics, not Stephanie.

FRESHMAN YEAR, EVERYONE on top of everyone. No space. All the people on her hall brushing their teeth in unison, buying posters with the discernment of gallerists, tumbling through the stairwells in a joyful stampede. The pile of the dormitory carpet, tight and thick with gossip from long-ago nights. Everything startling, immediate. Incredible. The smells. Disinfectant and cheap cologne, body butter, hair cream, stale beer, feet.

The academic buildings, large and brilliant with light. Or underground, no windows, a basement lab for a popular course, deep in the recesses of the hill. Broken chairs, and seminar tables, and lecture halls filled with haphazard benches and beams. Stephanie could learn everything wrong, and these classrooms would still make her feel close to being right. The nearness of knowledge, the earnestness of the pursuit, all overlapping. Knowing was not the same as wanting to know, but in college, maybe it was.

Stephanie's suitemate Doris, always awake. "Have you finished that paper?" people asked her.

"I'm possessed," Doris would say, "simply possessed," she'd say, sticking pencils in her hairdo.

People in college said shit like this all the time. "I'm possessed and on a mission!" Doris said at three o'clock in the morning.

Early morning, no one awake but Doris and Stephanie.

A lawn mower growling in the distance. The starlings that lived in the trees on the quad, rejoicing. The booming horn of Stephanie's dreams, driving her into daylight, into the shock of cold air through the window, a current cooling the sweat on her sheets.

After the second meeting of his bird-watching club (cardinal, finch, thrush), Will found Stephanie in the bathroom at dawn, deepening the shower stall into a tub.

"Oh," he said.

The lawn mower, sputtering.

"You can never tell. Please, don't tell." Stephanie made him promise. "Swear." In her bathrobe, her flip-flops. Whatever. Swear.

"I swear, I swear," he said.

Will had bushy eyebrows and deep-set eyes. He had bad posture and an endless supply of vintage T-shirts and jeans. But also, Stephanie had noticed him without a shirt, in the hall at night. He always looked concerned about something. He always had half a pack of ramen to share.

"It fits in the bowl better when you only use half," he explained to their suite, this scholar of soup.

"Promise," she said.

"Okay, I promise," Will said, but he had already seen things. The clogged sink, last Monday, jutting toward the window at an unlikely angle. His ramen bowl, without warning, big enough for a whole square of noodles.

Later, he wanted to know the limits. Could she create a new country, could she change her body. Did it hurt.

Stephanie had never considered this before. It did hurt. It was like a pulling or a pressure behind her eyes. Sometimes, afterward, she saw stars. She said this in a whisper. Their knees were touching. Look at how Will folded himself to fit next to her.

"But it's fine," she added, not wanting to sound too fragile.

"Of course," he said, nodding, like this was the most obvious thing in the world.

WILL—STEPHANIE'S VERY FIRST friend. He had a mind for politics and philosophy and pretty much all the subjects. Framed posters of French films from the sixties around his desk. A collection of music both corny and erudite. His furrowed brow, crinkling toward some distant inner city of knowledge. A guitar in the corner of his room, gathering dust. Aptitude like an armor.

"I took a class on that!" Will would say in response to most things.

When Will was older, he attended an office party in a high-rise with a coworker whose heart he was planning to break. She drank too much champagne that night because it stung—knowing he was finished with her before she could ever imagine being done with him. The woman found their boss and described Will with a vituperative flourish. Some of their colleagues gathered around to listen. "That's Will," she said, wrapping up her argument, "the most talented guy in your freshman dorm!"

She grabbed the wrong coat, took a cab home, not proud.

But that was much later. Here, in that freshman dorm,

Stephanie found Will perfect. She loved watching him talk about her predicament.

"Our predicament," he'd say.

He thought he knew everything. It was beautiful. Even Stephanie, who knew very little, knew that knowing a little was all anyone could hope for. And yet she could not resist the way he seemed to know a lot. His arrogance, every grammatical correction pressing on the words she would have used to describe her heart. Valedictorian from the Midwest. A kind of charm to which she was not immune. Her bed stretched from twin to full when he sat there on her pillows, strategizing.

"Did we just shrink, or did something grow?" Will asked.

Someone to share the predicament. Our predicament! The situation of her life. Sad, strange girl plus one. Not so lonely anymore. A small idea that grew. Friendship—a sudden shift in her perimeter.

"Are you allergic?" Will asked.

"Allergic to what?"

"You always pick them out of your food," he said, looking at her plate and forking the harvested slice of pepper. This close reading of her behavior was almost too much for Stephanie to comprehend. No one had ever bothered to track her movements and turn them into a story.

When everyone had left for a basement concert, Will knocked on Stephanie's door.

"Show me," he said. "If you want, I mean."

She took him to the far end of the hall, near the mi-

crowave, and closed her eyes when they reached the storage crawl space. The pulsing, the great ache rising easily
in his presence, spreading the plaster and stopping on a
possibility that Stephanie liked. That was how it always
started and ended, with potential.

She opened the door to reveal a tunnel, a secret mar-
gin that could fit one or two people side by side. They
wriggled down into the spot that Stephanie had invented,
just for them.

"I don't understand," Will said, looking up at the rotting beams. They were flat on their backs, and she could
feel the hairs on his arm against hers. "It doesn't make any
sense. Where are we?"

"I don't know," Stephanie said.

What are you thinking right now? she wanted to ask.
But then again, she much preferred not knowing what
was on his mind. There was more of her in the world, for
maybe being thought of by him.

"It reminds me of someplace," Will said. "It's so familiar."

With their arms barely touching, a new idea entered
the room. Something Stephanie hadn't considered before.

If she closed the tunnel behind them, where would
they go?

But Will was already sliding back down the hall, toward the stairs.

"I think I can still make it to the concert!" he said,
dusting off his pants.

Out of the tunnel, the crawl space retracting to its

original shape. Then back on her bed, all the heartache arrived. She wished she could make her room large enough to escape herself—pathetic! There must be a horizon at the edge of this feeling, Stephanie thought, but it was still out of view. She switched on her purple lamp and curled under the old quilt, the sound of happiness attacking from a distant quad. Oh, she could go everywhere in her life and still never make it to the end of Will.

The classrooms, the library, the cafeteria, the dorm. The sharp hexagon of her daily routine expanding in his presence, more prismatic, digressive, a creased and tented map. On the other side of the room, on the other side of his jokes, in his university-branded hat, in his circumference of recognition, at the terrible recital, under the famous courtyard statue, once again in the crawl space tunnel, and across from him on the couch in their suite. College was a series of meeting spots arranged across time, in proximity to trees. She waited for him to arrive by accident at the place she had picked on purpose.

Doris in the doorway.

"You guys good?" she asked. "I'm running on fumes. Possessed."

"Possessed," they agreed.

The three of them walked to a party in one of the houses off campus. Doris gave Stephanie her phone so that she would not send precious darlings.

"What's a precious darling?" Stephanie asked.

"You know, the kind of message you wish you hadn't

sent the night before," Doris said, laughing. "Like, kill your darlings."

"Oh, sure, no problem."

"You're saving my life. I'm in love with ten people right now, it's horrible," Doris said. She climbed over a table and vanished into the crowd.

The floor, littered with red cups. "Empties!" someone yelled. Stephanie stepped over the trash to find a place on the screened porch. A table, a chair, metal mixing bowls filled with vending machine food. There was beer, both pong and keg.

Stephanie kept accidentally blocking the door, standing in the flow of porch traffic.

"Yo, stop blocking the door!" a very drunk trio said in unison, hurtling out into the yard. Stephanie stepped aside and watched them collapse in the grass, laughing at their own stunt.

"Will, you have to see this!" someone yelled.

When she heard his name, a little alcove appeared at the center of the moment, a room where she could sit and be alone with him again.

"Come on," he said, from the room in her mind. But no, he was there, at the party. He grabbed Stephanie's arm and took her to join the crowd in the kitchen. Doris was performing on the countertop and lip-syncing to a popular song. But she had abandoned the lyrics halfway through, made up new words, ones that didn't match. A few more audience members joined the counter concert—"Toutes des flûtes!" someone trilled when the orchestra arrived. Several loners lingered together by the fridge.

"The kitchen is at capacity!" the host of the party yelled, distraught, her chest shiny with sweat. "I repeat, the kitchen is at capacity!"

"Then let's make it bigger!" Will shouted, and everyone cheered. He looked at Stephanie and she looked back at him, terrified.

"Why not?" he said, and she shook her head, her body falling against him.

"No, no, please, no, please," she said, squeezing his hands, on the verge of tears.

No one was watching or listening. The students had taken Will's suggestion to heart, and they were busy opening the windows, climbing onto the butcher block island, and charging through the remaining space. Doris tapped the ceiling with an umbrella but she did not have the muscle to do much harm. Other people did. A cabinet door fell off its bracket and the flutes were playing a prelude very badly. A prelude to what, unclear. Streakers streaked through every room.

"The kitchen is closed!" the host moaned. "I repeat, the kitchen is closed!" She blocked the door with a dramatic gesture, and Stephanie and Will ducked under her arm.

The best of nights always seemed to end like this, with an ousting. Or they didn't end at all—they just bumped into morning and kept ambling in the direction of lunch.

On the walk home, a fresh dew drenched the lawn, covered the bottoms of their jeans in damp splotches, blades of mown grass like embroidery over the denim. Stephanie and Will reviewed the events of the evening, cataloging who was drunkest, who was loudest, who was worthiest, and all the rest. The sudden retrospect of parties, a quirk of college, panning for nostalgia in the onslaught of the present. Over the field, a pyramid of shadows stretched and joined with voices somewhere even farther down the lawn. No bodies to be seen, just the suggestion of bodies. Will and Stephanie were still alone.

"But I wish you hadn't scared me like that," she said after the debriefing was done.

"Scared you?"

"Making the kitchen grow."

"Oh, come on," Will said, throwing an arm around her. He laughed. "An inside joke!"

"Yeah?"

"No one knew what I meant. No one knew, except for you. Hang on," he said. He made her wait by the pond, thinking he had heard a loon. They stood there listening, but loons were rare.

Stephanie was still upset. Then again, she had never been on the inside of a joke before. Other people had jokes about her, she was certain—Mr. Dougherty's class, the lockers, the cafeteria floor—but she was always stuck on that screened porch, trying to find a seat. It felt good, and she leaned into Will a little, the crook of his fleece accommodating her tank top and hoodie, a timorous courage accumulating where there had been none. Turning down the main college road, they didn't say a word. Will's hand resting on her shoulder. The light on the path pooled around them, giving way to an incredible dark at the corner with the broken lamp. The uncommon capacity of the smallest hours in the day. Everything was completely still, and Stephanie wished she could make moments bigger too. But of course, that was what memory was for.

She imagined her sister, on the other side of the world, feeling just as good. No—better. She was also walking home with someone she loved. Everything was clearer; the love was clearer too. There were loons nearby, and they were easy to find.

"It's so late!" Will said when they were back at the dorm. "Sweet dreams," he said over his shoulder, but he was already basically gone.

THE HOST OF the party in off-campus housing threw many other parties, over the years. In fact, at one point, this was her job. She organized the catering and the guest list and the microphones, if needed. She planned a corporate party in a high-rise for a nefarious company. Nefarious tippers, at least. Another, at the most famous restaurant in the city. Every now and then, she could see that very first college party peeking through the seams of the current party, like a guest trying to crash the event. The streakers, the girl lip-syncing on the counter, the busted cabinets. The sad girl wandering the screened porch, alone. The party host would never let someone wander around alone—not anymore. What an amateur mistake. She threw parties for her neighbors, for her friends, in her studio apartment, her chest glistening with sweat, leaning out onto the fire escape for a swish of breeze and not worrying about the mess in the kitchen, the broken vase near the couch. Once, her cheap table belly-flopped to the floor, flinging snacks toward every corner of the room. Weeks later, she was still laughing, delighting in the discovery of stray olives underfoot. No one would ever throw a party for the host, but this was what she preferred. If you sit on the edges of your own universe, you still might have been the center of someone else's.

AUTUMN BREAK AND Stephanie stayed at school. Parents' Weekend, no time to visit, Dad is cleaning the gutters this month, Mom has an important lunch. Thanksgiving in the basement meeting room with the other kids who could not make it home, who failed to assemble a road that led them back to where they had started. Stephanie loaded her tray with all the seasonal sides. Cheesy potatoes, green beans, corn from a can. One girl cried because she was missing her younger brother's homecoming game, but the train was too expensive this time of year. There were carpools, but gas was expensive too. For so long, the world had been trending toward convenience. That was over. People had barely noticed the shift, and yet, distance was growing brittle again, confusing and tedious to navigate. Stephanie walked the lonely dimensions of the campus, empty quads, quiet lobbies, silent recreation silos where she could be alone in the vacant halls and squares. And then, life returned student by student, a matrix of souls to populate the endless, obliterating space.

Stephanie called her parents, but no one answered. She left a message on their machine and pictured her voice filling the empty house. But no, the house wasn't empty. They were there, she knew, watching the phone. Not picking up.

THE DINING HALL, empty for a week, full again. Rooms getting bigger and smaller without help from Stephanie. A standing breakfast date with Will for the day after vacation, something to look forward to, he had written on her whiteboard the time and the place. She waited for him in a seat toward the far wall and poked at her western omelet. Outside, a game of Frisbee materialized on the lawn. One player's path revealed another player in the distance, and that player ran until she revealed the presence of two teams. Stephanie watched the disc soar, a candy shell arriving in an open palm, launched from the wrist of an invisible player who would never enter Stephanie's line of sight.

What would she tell him first? Which detail would reveal the presence of another detail? The sad affair of Thanksgiving, the way they had turned off the heat by accident in the dorm, a group of students amassed in the dimly lit curve of the campus center waiting for updates, Stephanie clutching her torso like a tree wrapped in its own branches. No, she would start with questions. She would let him talk about his extended family, the cousins spilling over onto the deck, his mother's gravy spilling on the tablecloth. She had hoped that he would invite her home with him but knew how far-fetched the idea sounded. Maybe if she asked the right question, it would bend across the events of the semester, revealing a bus to the Midwest with Will for the next break.

"That's not supported by evidence," Will said, from the room in her mind.

But no—he was here, in the cafeteria, at a crowded table near the condiments. The Frisbee knocked against the glass, startling Stephanie awake. She took her tray and went to join him, too surprised to wonder if she was welcome.

"I thought we were meeting for breakfast," Stephanie said.

"Stephanie! Join us," a girl said, and Will looked up, uncomfortable. He moved closer to the girl, nudging down the bench.

"Stephanie," the girl said, with her fingers on Will's elbow. She was wearing the kind of hat built for fashion, not weather. "You have to help us settle a debate."

"Okay," Stephanie said, and she squeezed between two student government wonks.

"Will posed a hypothetical to the group. If you could make the world bigger, would you do it?" She took her tray in her hands and motioned to suggest the tray, expanding.

"It's just a hypothetical," Will said, turning pale.

Stephanie had thought they would talk about Frisbee, family, turkey. She had imagined saving Will the red peppers from her western omelet. Maybe he would even put his hand on her shoulder again. Where had this imagined version of events gone now that something different was happening?

"It's not just hypothetical," a lacrosse player said, reaching over Stephanie for the salt. "You can't make something bigger without taking away from something else."

"Ah, an imperialist reading," Will said, looking at Stephanie for encouragement.

"No, it's a scientific reading," the lacrosse player said. "It's a matter of matter." He was delighted with this turn of phrase and shook some salt on Stephanie's eggs to underline his point. "It's a matter of matter," he said again, every September for thirty years, teaching physics to teenagers. The teenagers groaned.

"But making more of the world might *save* the world," the girl said with moony eyes, touching Will's elbow every time she spoke. "If we can make the world big enough, maybe it will never die."

"No," Doris said, looking out the window. Stephanie had not seen her sitting there at the end of the table. "Making the world bigger won't save it. It will just make it hurt worse when it's gone."

"I took a class on that!" Will said.

"No addition without subtraction," the student body treasurer said, taking a roll from Stephanie's tray to demonstrate his theory.

Stephanie thought of her little sister then, living her life on the other side of the planet, losing a molecule every time Stephanie made something grow. A feeling crumbled all around her. She looked at Will, who turned away and laughed at a joke happening down the length of the table. Stephanie pretended to hear it too, and smiled.

In all their late nights, with all his questions (so many questions!), he had never once asked her why. Why it happened, and when—he didn't care. Stephanie would have told him it was because of a craving, a longing, so deep inside her that it was outside her body. A place to put the wanting. Or maybe he didn't ask because he did not want to know the answer.

"HAS ANYONE SEEN Doris?" The resident adviser was looking for her, checking in all the rooms.

She had given Stephanie her phone again and had never come back to pick it up.

The suitemates looked under the couch, all over campus. They looked in her usual hiding places where she stayed up all night working.

Dead meat, Stephanie thought, sweating. She thought of all the pencils suspended in Doris's hair.

"Can't you do something?" Will whispered, his mouth near her neck. "Like sonar, like echolocation."

"I'm not a whale, for fuck's sake," Stephanie said.

The search spread from dorm to dorm and went into the night. All of them with flashlights, like that depressing Danish television program that everyone watched on Wednesdays. Doris was an episode behind, Stephanie remembered, a hard sadness coming up through her chest.

Illuminating the quad. The grass extending to the curb. They covered every inch.

Three o'clock in the morning.

When they found Doris in the back of the science building, she was unconscious. It was a locked room that no one even knew existed, filled with comfortable chairs and rare texts about marine life. They had to call maintenance to open the door. Then the ambulance.

"Why do you have her phone?" the man from campus security asked Stephanie.

Will watched her from across the hall.

"Something about precious darlings," Stephanie mumbled. "She was always saying. She was in love."

"Okay, thanks. We'll take that," he said, and Stephanie put the phone in his palm.

Everyone on campus wanted to know about Doris. Famous overnight. Legend.

"Remember how she used to be like, *I'm possessed*?" someone said on the front steps of the library. They went quiet when Stephanie walked by. Everyone went quiet when Stephanie entered the common room to grab a movie from the shelf. Will looked up at her, briefly, checking a blind spot, then down at his lap.

The student government wonks walked hand in hand, then divided around Stephanie's approach. Stephanie, in the line of the Frisbee's projected flight. But no one ran in her direction or opened their arms for her to toss it back into play. A new Frisbee was produced. The one that landed near Stephanie's feet, abandoned.

Campus in winter was half melting, half freezing. The pine trees hung heavy with collisions of ice, like glass-ware smashed in midair and suspended. To the concert hall, alone. Everywhere alone. What a shame, to have less, after briefly having more. One bassoon solo that made Stephanie pay attention. The notes rising through a buzz-ing orchestration, continuing up and drifting above the melody into a new key, then off the scale as if into a dif-ferent composition, without a resolution to be found.

Stephanie swam laps in the old gymnasium, and she increased the size of her lane just a little bit. No witnesses, extra space to keep her company. Now, her world abruptly diminished, she found the old inclination, wanting to ex-ist somewhere beyond the boundaries of herself. The wa-ter shifted in the pool, changing volume.

It wasn't until she finished that she saw them look-ing at her. The diving team in the balcony, staring and baffled. She pulled down her goggles, could see their large eyes from a distance, communicating confusion and something more.

"It's just like he described it," she could hear the div-ing captain say, almost smiling. The shock and delight of a rumor confirmed.

"You told," she said.

"Told what?" Will was snuggled on his bed with the girl from the horrible breakfast. Stephanie had opened his door without knocking and the girl's laughter emptied from the room.

"You told everyone."

"Hold on, hold on," Will said to the girl, frowning. Then, "You're blocking the door, Stephanie."

"Sorry," Stephanie said. She stepped aside and followed him into the hall. People passing on their route to dinner. And how very far away from her he stood. Practically pressed against the opposite wall. "Could we go somewhere more private?" she asked.

"This is good."

"Hey, Will," the girl in his room yelled. "Do you have some sweatpants I can borrow?"

"In the bottom drawer," he yelled back.

"Does she know too?" Stephanie asked.

"I'm not sure what you were expecting."

"So you did tell everyone."

"You can't just mess with people's lives like that," Will said, rubbing his eyes. "I had to say something. It was a question of safety, you see."

"I don't understand," Stephanie said.

"After everything that happened with Doris. The secret room," he said, but Stephanie looked at him blankly. "You don't even know yourself. It's so obvious."

It wasn't obvious. For a brief and hopeful moment, Stephanie thought that maybe this would be an instance of clarity, a translucent memory that she could look through like a loupe to make sense of her entire life.

"Please. What do you mean?"

"No, I'm not going to spell it out for you," he said, but then he did it anyway. "I heard what happened to your sister. It's a pattern," he whispered. "You need help. *Real help.*"

Stephanie looked at Will but couldn't see him anymore. Pressure behind her eyes and curls of pain.

"I'm just saying this as a friend." Will exhaled with the kind of exhaustion she did not know she inspired in him.

I can't believe you told, Stephanie thought. But that wasn't why she was upset. Was that really the worst crime, or was it that Will didn't love her back? He had given her a sturdy grievance, and in a way, she was thankful for it. Now she could build a little reason in her heart to hate him, something that was his fault, not hers.

"Are we done here?" Will asked, exhaling again. But she saw it wasn't exhaustion. His hands were clenched against his sides. Another group of students walked through their confrontation on the way to dinner, and when they passed, his palms released. His posture relaxed. In the hallway, he had witnesses. Stephanie realized that Will was afraid.

She must have run from him then, because when she looked around, she was no longer in the dorm. Snow swirling in great movements of havoc, falling up and rising down. On the open green, through the crisp grass like burgeoning stubble on a chin, holding herself against the chill. Stephanie was not sure—was the mud suddenly deep because her thoughts were stretching into the earth or because of the melting slush? On the other side of the world, her sister was up to her ankles in mud too, but for happy reasons. She was planting a garden, Stephanie decided, wading through the soil, her pants cuffed around her calves, flinging seeds through her fingers, laughing at a joke that someone she loved had told her earlier in the day.

Stephanie sat on the ground to be closer to the other side of the world. There, she calmed herself in the cyclone of flurries. If only she could see around her own corners. Her internal architecture, in constant disrepair. Stone buildings on the great lawn, bright and imposing, dressed in their glamorous evening lighting. What was the occasion? Oh yes. She had lost her only friend. So comfortable looking forward to him—the promise of the future had marbled the surface of her present. She could not pick apart the moment, the order of events. It had already happened, but it was also still happening. And she would sometimes remember it wrong, because it hadn't happened yet.

In the morning, the groundskeeping crew stood around a muddy, deep cavity on the lawn, shaking their heads. They had to phone a contractor, put the work form through the office, and wait for a shipment of seeded soil, blocked out into neat tiles. Probably an animal, they said. Kids are animals.

DORIS RETURNED TO campus. A welcome-home party. She sat on the couch grinning, then wandered back to her room. She wanted things calm, quiet. Her ears, always ringing. Stephanie was sitting on the floor in their hall, stood to greet her. Strange girl, Doris thought, always her eyes rimmed with something bad. On the verge of something. In love with that dumb boy Will in the room next to the microwave. Even when Will ignored her, Stephanie would count it as attention. Doris knew something about this tendency, and it made her warm to Stephanie for a moment.

She nodded and went to her room. Then she swung her head back out into the hall.

"It was pills, by the way," Doris said. "I don't know why I'm telling you."

"Oh," Stephanie said.

"I don't know why you throw a kegger for someone who's newly sober, but." Doris shrugged. She half smiled, then closed her door and went to sleep.

After graduation, Doris found out about the rumors, evil Stephanie, crone, villain, creating space where there was none. Creating a secret room above the science center, locking Doris inside.

"Are you fucking kidding me?" Doris said, her fingers on her temples. Her friends looked shaken.

"We didn't know what to think!" they said. "You were always saying you were possessed. And Stephanie—"

"I was on drugs. My god." Doris explained about the

secret room, donated by a wealthy alum. "He was supposed to meet me there, and never—" Doris swallowed.
"Precious darlings, you know."

She tried to get in touch with Stephanie many years
later but couldn't find a phone number that worked. It was
like she had vanished from the face of the earth. Some
people are never as interesting as they are in those first
months of college. Not true for Doris. There was a string
of highly publicized affairs—the style editor, the CEO,
the actress with the series of blockbusters about antelope,
long extinct (the antelope, not the actress—though one
review argued the reverse). And then Doris went on to
become famous in certain circles for her fearless memoir, *Darlings,* about those years in her early twenties when
each object had a fantastic halo of light, nothing made
sense, and she was high every day of her life.

Stephanie graduated. Finished early. Forever a part
of campus lore. Like their old school mascot, the crow,
long extinct. Urban legends both. Strange girl, sitting on
the steps of Philosophy Hall. That was the picture in the
yearbook, anyway. She saved and bought a ratty car from
a man with three first names, and drove and drove, filled
her gas tank with the cheapest fuel and kept driving.
Those were the years when she was in constant motion
without care for appointments or ambition.

Her sister rotated along the opposite side of the world,
a road trip with friends, leaning through her sunroof, sing-

ing. Keeping the distance between them taut and constant.

There were places you could stop and take pictures, and for this Stephanie made time. She stopped and hiked the Grand Canyon. So much space, an endless buffet of texture and shadow. She selected a red pebble, slipped it in the pocket of her dress, which she had purchased at the only worthwhile secondhand store in the state. The strata layered from sediment to igneous rock, the tectonic story of the world. Stephanie considered the shifting plates of her own minor universe, how she had learned to lift herself through space in far fewer than billions of years. Red rock to redwoods. Trees so tall they scratched the ozone without any help from Stephanie. The rings around the stumps, endless. Ancient.

The Great Lakes, enormous. She could mess with the edges of the muck, and no one would ever guess, no one would know. The Mall of America. Enormous. Only landmarks, only the big ones. Badlands, Mount Rushmore, bridges, no particular order.

When traveling it was typical to keep in touch, and so Stephanie tried her best to follow the rules. A call or a postcard to her parents, every now and then. A photo of Stephanie, diminished in the spray of a geyser. Smaller and smaller in the rearview mirror.

"Be safe," her dad said on the phone.

"Okay."

But he wasn't worried about her safety. He was worried about everyone else.

"Mom says hello."

When Stephanie needed money, she slept in her car, or she stopped in a town and worked odd jobs for women with names like Tiny and at stores with names like No Good News. She separated the jobs into their shapes and spaces. The lozenge of blue nail polish painted on the side of the cash register. The slices of zucchini in the summer pie. The globular cheese at the back of the market fridge. The radii of the window booths, the kind with wraparound red vinyl seats, filled with kids who had nothing to do, nowhere to be.

Every now and then she arrived in a place where her desire lifted and arced toward an invisible promontory in her heart. The tourist attraction. The field near the edge of town. The creeks and gas station markets, the grottoes and parking lots, the spots on the map that had mutable boundaries. Locations where she was tempted to break through some old illusion of geography and leave her mark, a yearning swelling in her foundation. Stephanie could not say whether the places called to her or whether the call came from somewhere invented. Whether she left the landscape changed or noticed an already existing possibility that no one else could see.

In one motel, two doors opened into separate rooms, creating a forty-five-degree angle at the end of the hallway. It was a wild bit of real estate—the Madison girl would've called it "a charming feature"—you could not open one door without blocking the other, and so, the guests in those rooms could never be together. Stephanie did not change its measurements. Funny. It looked the way she felt, forever out of step with the whole wide world.

YEARS VANISHED IN a familiar way. The chores, the small empty things. The groceries, the laundromat, the hourly shifts, the trip from here to there, but never back. The events that happened across months and formed a single continuous memory, erasing larger units of time. A bag of gathered minutes tossed over a ledge.

THE TRANSGRESSIONS ACCUMULATED too. The diner where they asked Stephanie about the hidden pantry, the one that had not come with the lease. The motel, yes, where she returned to change the measurements. How could they let those doors slam against each other for eternity? It wasn't right. But our property will be assessed, the owner said, holding the door open for Stephanie to scram. The national park where the rangers suddenly had more terrain to attend to, more nature than they had agreed to preserve.

SHE DREAMED OF a damp cave. There were a thousand entrances, but only one exit. She had left the cave many years ago, she knew. If she could only remember this, then she would find her way out again. And yet, each time she came upon an entrance, she forgot that she had ever wanted to leave.

STEPHANIE LANDED IN a city. Expensive, anonymous. Her corner smelled like trash even after the trash was collected every Tuesday. The woman on the first floor moaned all day and all night. Stephanie vowed to never make space again. Only in private, only within the four walls of her apartment. Invisible space, invisible just like Stephanie. A deeper mug for coffee, an extra inch of fridge. No one to make her world bigger. No one to hurt. She applied for secretarial positions and worked in obscurity. She was a puff of air emitted from someone accelerating in the opposite direction.

If you had asked about Stephanie around this time, people would have said that she was a very hard worker. Smart. Too smart? Punctual, proactive. A waste of talent, maybe, one boss would have said, if you had asked her. The boss noticed something about Stephanie, something sad and distant. Dangerous? No. She searched for her online and found nothing but half stories. Graduated early, home was far away. Some photos from a road trip. Only landscapes in the photos, only Stephanie, alone.

"I'm taking you under my wing," her boss said one afternoon.

"You don't have to do that," Stephanie said.

"It's okay, there's room for you there."

"Really, I don't need anything. It's fine."

"Too late. Here, collate these for me? My wings have many documents that need filing." Stephanie's boss winked and walked away.

The office radiator sang in the winter and the air conditioner clacked in the summer. The desks were all the same desk, all matching and purchased as a set with the chairs and the cabinets, a satisfying, coordinated atmosphere. Stephanie had the same laminate desk as the receptionist, as the PR lead with his big head of curls, as her boss. She had the same desk as Annie the sales associate. Annie had a thermos and a pastry on the corner of her desk every morning, and sometimes she left a pastry on the corner of Stephanie's desk too.

"Sustenance!" she said, smiling. Stephanie smiled. Then they both laughed.

The way Annie laughed reminded Stephanie of her little sister, cheeks and open mouth, with very little sound. But no—her sister was on the other side of the world, typing an opposite letter for every letter that Stephanie typed, her desk exactly the same as Stephanie's, only backward.

Now her sister was an adult, and Stephanie could feel, even in her imagination, a disagreement flowering between them. Was she typing opposite letters or opposite ideas? For everything Stephanie believed, her sister believed something else. The gravity still held them afloat, but it was a hostile orbit, a conflict at its core. They were growing apart, in unison.

"CAN YOU BELIEVE they don't have paid maternity leave?" one of Annie's friends said to Stephanie in outrage. They were decorating for Annie's baby shower, and she helped fill balloons to scatter them across a table in the stranger's house. Circumferences expanding, just air, no funny business. Jelly beans in honey bears. Streamers and cupcakes and gifts. Annie arrived and laughed silently in the doorway, her cheeks turning pink. Her husband dropped her off and waited in the car outside for a minute before pulling away.

Then the dolls and diapers and learning toys. The bowl filled with advice.

Annie picked a folded card.

"'Always make room for yourself!'" she read.

"It's so important," one of the women said, her face full of emotion in the presence of her own words. Some silent nodding and hands on hearts.

"Oh. This one's blank," Annie said, holding up another card. It was Stephanie's.

Then the desserts and juice and baffling tales of birth. Two women competed for the worst labor, and two others competed for the best child. Stephanie wanted to live somewhere in the middle of things, not worst, not best, just here. But the sheer abundance of stories only drew attention to how very little she had to say. She felt blurry, went to the toilet and lingered there. Looked at the lotions lined around the sink. So many scents and purposes. Preventative, restorative, calming, cooling. How to escape this party. Expanded the medicine cabinet until she saw stars, a pressure behind her eyes, almost passed out.

"There you are!" Annie said, finding Stephanie returning from the bathroom. Annie grabbed both of her hands conspiratorially. "Did you try the cupcakes?"

"Red velvet," Stephanie said, her stomach turning. "Delicious."

"Oh, come on, red velvet isn't even a real flavor." Annie grinned fiercely, making a mock-evil laugh under her breath.

"It's true, someone could've splurged for Funfetti."

"This is awful. I hate being the center of attention," Annie said. "I hate baby shit. Please don't abandon me!"

"I won't," Stephanie said, smiling, Annie's hands still in hers. Her little sister's chubby hands.

"Listen," Annie said, snatching a glass of lemonade from the table. "They need someone to cover my clients while I'm away. I told them it should be you."

"Oh, no. Thanks, no. That's up to the boss."

"She agrees with me! She loves you," Annie said. "She practically wants to adopt you."

Stephanie looked startled.

"Oh, you're not adopted, are you?" Annie asked.

"No," Stephanie said. She thought of her parents, whether she could really claim them as her own anymore. Two small remnants, like porcelain figurines abandoned on the floor of her mind.

"I'm so sorry," Annie said. "My parents are dead! I don't know how to talk about things."

"That's terrible," Stephanie said.

"No, the cupcakes are terrible. Keep up, keep up."

"Okay, I will." Stephanie smiled.

"Hey, do me a favor," Annie said. "Forget everything I ever say, will you?"

"Sure," Stephanie said, already remembering the conversation better than Annie ever would.

"Come, let's play pin the baby on the diaper or whatever the fuck."

The other women blindfolded Annie and spun her around in a circle. Stephanie watched Annie rotate, hectic and stumbling. Her jaw fell. This was what she experienced, always, plummeting through space. She had never seen it before, acted out so perfectly. Each revolving wobbly loop. Yes, Stephanie thought, yes, exactly. Then Annie pinned the diaper to the baby, and everyone cheered.

STEPHANIE TOOK GOOD care of Annie's clients. It had been so long since someone believed in her ability to do right. Do well. Adult rules. Everything had finite measurements and could be assessed objectively.

"You're doing great," her boss said, tapping on her desk whenever she walked by.

Stephanie stayed late and arrived early. Walking past the intersection that smelled like trash every day of the year. The tenant downstairs in her building had stopped moaning and Stephanie wondered if she had finally recovered, or finally died. She lingered outside the woman's apartment, listening for signs of life, picturing a gruesome scene just on the other side of the door.

But no. No more. On with her day, in her black boots and matching socks. She was responsible, in her coat that matched the forecast, and she hoped someone would notice. The adult world was brighter. A punctual longitude, latitude. A train car the size of a train car. A commute that never took longer than it should. At least never because of Stephanie. Everything the size it had always been, always would be. Predictable. Put a foot out into the air and trust it to find the stair it's looking for.

Stephanie had located a kind of harmony, as quiet and small as it was. A proportional way to live. Now the branch of her elm was always where she needed it to be. The sunlight spilled through her single window at the same angle every morning. Always make room for yourself! It's so important. She sometimes ordered a medium soup from her local joint, the broth perfectly portioned in its cup. It was peaceful, a waltz, a procession of existing, with no detours, no hidden places, nothing beyond what the eye could see.

"Is it really you?" Will asked from the room where she still sometimes visited him in her mind.

But no—he was there, at the counter, holding a sandwich and waiting to pay.

Will's face was kinder, thicker than before. The missing years, accumulating around his shoulders, a fissure in her afternoon. The world swelled to accommodate his arrival.

"Oh!" she said, and put her hand over her mouth.

She had been following her rules. No extra space, for anyone. But of course, it had been easy. No desire. Stephanie had not longed for anything in ages.

"Let me," he said. He paid for her soup, and the cabinet under the cash register ballooned around its woodwork.

"It's good to see you," she said, touching his wrist, then quickly pulling away.

"I heard you lived nearby, but I wasn't sure."

He was on a trip for work, no return ticket yet, or so he said. They walked with their lunches. She imagined that soon he would have somewhere else to be, and the anticipation of his departure was hot on the back of her neck. A redness bloomed across her chest. The sun, still warm before retreat, glowing on slick pavement, and they walked through the shimmering bronze shapes that stretched across the intersection, down the main street, and beyond.

They fumbled through a conversation. The extinctions, the weather, its instability, the reports of fragment seasons: cusp spring, sudden autumn, and a new one called middle winter. Will asked Stephanie about her life since graduation, and she rearranged her time on the road to make it sound like an adventure. Stephanie tried to catch Will's eye, but he looked away. That was okay. It allowed her to behold him with the full force of her emotions. His hair, less. His posture, more.

"So the thing is . . ." Will said.

Stephanie did not move.

"I should say something about it," Will said. He laced his fingers and unwove them, pressed his palms to his thighs. They had finished their lunches on the bench, and Stephanie waited to hear what was next. She hoped he would express remorse, bury his face in his hands, or suggest that they dissect everything that had happened. Claim the blame, relieve her of blame. He balled his sandwich wrapper into an aluminum-and-paper clump.

"I feel regret," she imagined him saying, "so much regret."

"Me too," she would say, then a passing mention of Doris, recognition of the assumptions he had made.

"I'm sorry." A room in Will's mind, as he'd describe it, just like the one in hers, where for all these years, he had visited Stephanie.

And that's where Stephanie's imagination had gone without notice, to the room in her mind, down a flight of stairs, a deeper register of conversation. She could hear the things she hoped to hear, until the moment caved in on itself, which it always did. Stairs squeezing into a tight packet. Every word inaudible. From there, Stephanie could find another room, more of a foyer, that led her back to the surface of the lived moment.

"I wish I knew what to say," Will said.

She watched their conversation dissolve upon contact with reality. A truck honked, and Will shrugged. From his pocket he produced a dessert for them to share. She realized that in his view he had apologized, or offered something loving, when in fact, he had not offered anything at all. He looked contrite, which was perhaps not enough, but Stephanie decided that it was. She had filled the missing moment with something of her own invention. A donation made to life's inadequate plot.

Her sister, on the opposite side of the world, only a splintered fragment of Stephanie, caught in a breeze and tumbled off to some imaginary realm.

"And then. We never got to talk again," Will finally said. He met her eyes and pressed a bit of cookie between his forefinger and thumb.

"God, I really don't have the energy for this right now," her sister said. Her angry face reflected upside down in the wet sidewalk's sheen.

"Is THIS WHERE you live?" he asked. They saw each other a few more times before Will went home with Stephanie, past the trash corner and up the seven flights of stairs. He was stroking the arm of her couch, where the fabric was shredded and worn through to a yellow foam.

"This is my situation," she said. "The rent is good."

"Can't you make it bigger?" he asked, smirking at her.

"No, no, I don't do that anymore," she said, embarrassed. She brushed against his shoulder walking to the fridge, grabbed two cold cans from the shelf. They drank the beers quickly and Will went back to his hotel.

"You can stay longer," she offered.

"Early meetings."

The next time he came over, he followed her into the

kitchen and held her from behind, resting his chin on the back of her head. He did this a few more times, and other times, he didn't go near her at all. Just the couch and the beer and early meetings. Then there was the night when she made tea, and his hands finally moved down around her waist, then lower, slowly leading her across the room. He unbuttoned her top.

All his combined visits were one whole memory for Stephanie, and she wondered later if they had ever been separate evenings at all, or if she had stretched Will across the story to make him last longer.

"Here," he said, helping her lift an arm out of its sleeve. But maybe that had happened sooner?

Stephanie couldn't believe he was touching her. Even in her dreams, where the odds were pretty good, he only wanted her less than half the time.

He asked her again, pressed to her body, on the rug. She could feel him growing against her. He wanted to know. Can't you make it bigger. Anything. Me, you, us. Show me. His fingers combed through the underside of her hair, raking the strands out and away. I miss when you used to show me.

"I can't," she said.

"Just once," he said, kissing her forehead, leaving his mouth open against her skin.

And then she did. She wanted to, for him. He had rescued her. She remembered the Aegean Sea, a lost explorer with no atlas. Marooned. She had thrown herself into oblivion but now he was here. Come find me, she had cried in the most private part of her heart. He had found her. You are here. He was wrapped around her. She took the rug and made it move, the chevron pattern spreading. He thrust into her then, his mouth warm against her neck, a feeling inside him growing, expanding into something that, no matter how large, would always remain unseen.

WHEN ANNIE RETURNED to the office, the world was slightly bigger than before. Stephanie had already broken her own rules at least a dozen times. She had enlarged the cupboards in her kitchen until they hit the ceiling and the floor, and Will stared in amazement. Walk-in cupboards! he said, tackling her on her frameless bed, kissing her breasts and moving down past her belly. He had extended his stay indefinitely. His work was flexible, kind of like Stephanie.

"I don't want to leave, not yet," he said, holding himself up on a pillow next to her. Had she ever occurred to him before now? It didn't matter. He had occurred to her thousands of times, the recurring event of her life. It was unreal, Stephanie thought, the way a longing, remembered, could become a premonition. She took a jewelry box from her nightstand and enlarged its dimensions, the colorful glass lid throwing back sunlight in new configurations, flecking Will's face with gold and orange and green.

"No one else can do what you can do," he said.

"We don't know that."

At dinner with Annie and Edward, Stephanie was in

a daze. The fog of being loved had descended around her body and everything was slow-motion, a Jell-O mold barely settled. Settled. What would that mean? Look at this life, this family, their bed next to the oven, their brand-new dining table, their chairs, and their baby, bouncing on her father's knee. The world, a curated collection of things to want. Stephanie had not considered her options.

Annie ran back and forth around the room, welcoming Stephanie, offering her a drink, babbling about the size of the apartment, how small it was. Edward, making jokes about a closet stuffed with diapers. The white noise of their frenzy and embarrassment lapped against Stephanie in pleasant waves. Nothing entered her ears for longer than a second. She smiled at each thing they did, noticed the supermarket pastries on the countertop, the ones that ornamented Annie's desk every morning. A laugh overtook her lungs. Her heart looked for a place to put everything it could not hold, palms outstretched, creating an alcove to save her happiness for later. And there it was, the brief and familiar blurring of her senses. When she took the closet doorknob in her hand, the terrace appeared fully formed, as if dropped from some other world entirely. Stephanie seized with pain, tremors twisting behind her eyes. She did not even know what she had done until it was too late.

The looks on their faces. The absolute joy on their faces.

Stephanie walked around the terrace, pretending at nonchalance, pressure accumulating and radiating around her head.

"Shit, what a great space," she said. She was congratulating herself! She had never created something so large, so complete. There was an umbrella and a grill and twinkling lights. Vines scaling the wrought iron balustrade. Had she grown those too, somewhere inside her soul? Annie and Edward, for their part, acted as if nothing remotely unusual had happened. Annie told the story about the broker's fee, and so on, and so on. Rose babbled in approval.

They sat on the terrace for hours, refilling their glasses and plates. In fact, Stephanie noticed that the longer they stayed on the terrace, the more solid it felt underfoot. Rosie was breathing heavily against Edward's chest, and Annie looked blissfully calm, her bangs fluttering with each rush of cool air. And yes, the way the breeze felt on Stephanie's arms, sending chills down her spine, the way it carried a soft ocean smell up and over her face.

Stephanie helped them bring the dishes to the sink at the end of the night. She watched Edward and Annie, their covert glances. They thought they had discovered something new, but Stephanie had introduced them to something old.

"What fun. Especially this girlie," Stephanie said, heading to the street, tugging at Rose's foot.

"Thanks for making the trip," Edward said.

"Next time, you come to me!" Stephanie said. She imagined the woman on the first floor, the moaning, which had recently started up again. She imagined Edward sitting on the collapsed side of her sofa where the foam had gone flat.

"Of course we will," Annie said, wrapping Stephanie in a hug.

When Annie invited Stephanie over a few weeks later, Stephanie knew why. It didn't bother her. Who could blame them? She remembered the hug, which was warm, genuine. She could give them this gift, retract it, continue giving it. It cost her nothing, which was good. Free was good.

"These people are not your friends," Will said to her. She took a bag of salad, dumped it in a bowl. "They only want you to make space in their small, stupid lives," he said.

"That's unfair," Stephanie said. "I feel sorry for them."

"They're just using you. Can't you see that?"

"Annie was nice to me long before I had anything she wanted. I was nobody. Lonely. It's complicated."

"What do *you* want?"

"We could do what they did, maybe," Stephanie whispered, looking down at the salad. So quiet, she wasn't sure whether the words had even come out at first. "A little place. A family."

He smiled, but with a frown on the other side of the expression. He held her then, tightly, so tightly she forgot he hadn't responded to a single word she'd said.

STEPHANIE LET ANNIE and Edward take her friendship in the way they wanted to take it, over and over again. She tried on their life for size, playing house. It didn't matter why they needed her. She liked it. She liked being needed, being invited and included. Every time the terrace appeared, their faces. Even the baby, Rose, so sweet and sticky cheeked. They trusted her with their daughter. When they weren't looking, Stephanie stretched Rose's playpen, wider, wider, making Rose laugh and laugh. Stephanie never held Rose too close to the edge of the terrace. She was in control. She would not drop her, hugging her to her chest, making the grass grow to meet her, again and again.

Will left town for work and would return in the spring. He promised. Stephanie made him swear, just like in the bathroom of their dormitory all those years ago. She could wait for him a little longer.

In the meantime, she tried Annie's family on for size. Even Edward was appealing, his broad toothy grin and his inspired cooking. He would put a palm on the small of Stephanie's back as if to say, Come, we're over here. Join us. Annie would put an arm over Stephanie's shoulders, and Edward would dance with them together. They spent Thanksgiving and then New Year's Eve on the terrace, joking, singing, watching fireworks in the distance. Where were they? When were they? It didn't matter. Edward kissed Stephanie on the cheek, and she glowed.

Annie and Edward had endless anecdotes—their whirlwind vacation to Italy, their celebrity friend who lived on a private island, their reluctant involvement in a fraught inheritance battle.

"Terrace Stories," Edward whispered, when Annie went inside to get more snacks.

"What?" Stephanie said.

"They're like little fables. Little fibs. Don't tell Annie that I told you!" He laughed, and refilled her drink. "You should do one next. It's fun."

Stephanie listened to their Terrace Stories and wondered which parts were true. The truth was overrated, she realized. Knowing that certain parts were fiction, this was what filled her body with an unexpected warmth. It was love, to recognize the inventions and inconsistencies that make a person whole.

When the toilet was broken, Edward peed off the edge of the terrace, and she laughed along. No one had ever used the bathroom in front of Stephanie before, not even outdoors. She threw her head back and pretended to join in the fun.

"Gross, babe!" Annie said, and Stephanie was embarrassed by how much affection she felt for them right then.

Eddie, she said, instead of Edward. The jettisoned letters, the closeness they produced, the shape of the friendship shifted to fill a new name. Rosie, she said.

She hoped she would lose a few letters from her name, but they still called her Stephanie.

She was infatuated with everything. Soon, Will would come back to her. And she was in love with Annie's family. Why not admit it? At her desk, more clients, more responsibility. She worked with a smile on her face, slough-ing off the years that had made no sense. She had spent her life missing instructions to a world happening just in the next room. Stephanie walked the street and extended the branch of a tree down to meet her hand, to pluck a leaf and stick it in her hair. Who cared if someone saw? She wanted to be seen. Not marooned, not invisible. Large, inevitable, present.

HER SISTER ON the other side of the world, was she happy too? The one thing that kept her up at night. Stephanie imagined a terrace somewhere on an opposite longitude, where her sister sat feeling a breeze, the same breeze that had just wrapped around Stephanie's own shoulders. Maybe her sister's terrace was real, or maybe someone else had made space for her existence.

"I don't have to always do what you say I'm doing," her sister said, dismantling the terrace with a swipe of her hand.

"You can do whatever you'd like," Stephanie said.

"What I'd like," her sister said, "is to be alone in my thoughts, not alone in yours."

Stephanie tumbled through their argument until she landed somewhere outside of time, in sleep.

AT WORK, ANNIE'S desk had been moved to a different floor, and Stephanie went to bring her a pastry. But Annie wasn't there—she wasn't near the copy machine either. Her cubicle was empty. The email had arrived only moments before, announcing the changes in staffing, announcing Annie's departure and Stephanie's sales accomplishments. *Farewell* was a word, and *clients* was another, landing on Stephanie with density and volume.

Stephanie did not know that she had been taking Annie's clients. Did she? Her job—that wasn't what she had meant to do. She walked to the elevators, embarrassed, and saw Annie standing there, wiping her nose on her sleeve. A box of books, a plant under her arm. Annie looked away.

"I just heard," Stephanie said. "Listen. I'm so sorry."

Annie pressed the button again to call the elevator, trying to hold something back. Tears, or maybe something worse. She pressed it once more.

"Are you leaving now too?" Annie asked.

"Yeah, I was just about to head out." A lie. Stephanie's heart was racing. No wonder she had been so happy. She had been taking, and taking, and taking. No addition without subtraction. *Ah, an imperialist reading.* Stephanie wondered if her rare moments of happiness had always been siphoned away from someone else. There were people, she knew, whose happiness was exponential. They made the world happier just by being happy in it. Her sister—probably that kind of person.

"You should come over," Annie said.

"Really? Right now?"

"Now," Annie said, holding the door.

Standing in the elevator with Annie, Stephanie wished she could make some extra space, just a signal between friends. A white flag. But no, that would give too much away. Stephanie could feel Annie's cold glare, their silence contained and amplified and spun in circles. She wanted to bang on the walls or smack the emergency button, her eyes welling with an unexpected feeling of loss. She wanted the perfect word, the right sentence that would make Annie laugh silently, her cheeks round and red. Annie caught Stephanie staring at her from the other side of the elevator and Stephanie looked away. She understood that Annie needed her in this moment. But only for the terrace. It was good to be needed, even if it was for the wrong reasons.

"Can I carry your box?" Stephanie asked.

"No," Annie said.

"I COULD COME home to visit," Stephanie said, on the phone with her dad.

"Oh, we wouldn't want to cause you any trouble." His voice was anxious and wavery.

"It's no trouble. It might be nice."

"But the air travel," her dad said enigmatically, as if planes were a thing that existed only in history books.

"I have a little bit of money saved," Stephanie said.

There was no response, just the sound of dead space.

"Is Mom home?"

"She says hello."

IF YOU HAD asked someone about the world around this time, they might have shown mild concern. "It's a matter of matter," the lacrosse player said to his science class. He wasn't a lacrosse player anymore, and was it a matter of matter? He did not know. He was teaching toward the statewide exams and wasn't wondering about this particular problem. He was back together with David and wanted to get things right. They were planning a vacation to Hawaii after the school year was done. They were going to swim with whatever sea mammals were left to swim with, damn it. Other people were planning vacations too. The first inkling of disaster had already arrived, instigated itself into the corners of the plot, but no one knew where to look.

IN SPRING, WILL returned, just as he'd promised he would. Stephanie had cleaned the apartment. Made him brownies from a box, for later. What would he tell her first? Which detail would reveal the presence of another detail?

She met him at a coffee shop, where he was commiserating with a woman, a little bit older. They were both wearing stylish shoes and expensive suits. She was glad she had dressed up. She pulled her hair forward and then let it fall back, adjusting her pants and her blouse, catching her own eye in the window before meeting them inside. Her sister, somewhere beyond her reflection, clocking her expression in a mirror, thousands of miles away.

"Hi, I don't think we've been introduced," Stephanie said.

"Sorry for the ambush!" Will said. "This is someone I work with. She really wanted to meet you."

"Oh, hello," Stephanie said. "I love your coat."

"Thanks," the woman said. "It's not mine. I took the wrong one home from a party, would you believe."

"Ridiculous that you haven't returned it yet," Will said, shaking his head.

The woman ignored Will and smiled at Stephanie.

"I've heard so much about you," she said. She had a notebook and a pen on the table.

"Only good things, I hope," Stephanie said, laughing.

"Yes, amazing things," the woman said, and Stephanie blushed.

"Well then I'm sure Will exaggerated," Stephanie said. She was nervous, but this was good. Will was introducing her to the people in his life. She ordered a frivolous funny drink with whipped cream, and they talked about Will, their shared history and the valences of this mutual character in their lives. Stephanie was surprised because there did not seem to be very much overlap. She kept expecting to chime in with agreement, or to offer a footnote to the woman's stories that would lead through a gate toward some common territory. But each anecdote ended in a place Stephanie had not anticipated, leaving her feeling chilled and very much alone.

"Yes, exactly," she said when the woman described Will's playing a mean game of squash. Stephanie had never seen Will hold a racket or play a sport of any kind.

"I know we should probably do more small talk," the

woman continued, "but I'm just so excited to be here, meeting you. I am so thrilled that you want to work with us."

"Work with you?" Stephanie looked at Will, but he was already interrupting his friend. Was she a friend?

"No, no," Will said, "nothing has been agreed on yet."

"Of course not," the woman said. "I put the horse before the zebra. Are there still zebras? Everything is up to you, Stephanie. Naturally."

She cringed when she heard her name in this stranger's mouth. Oh, what a cliché she was, thinking people can ever do anything but the same verb over and over until the end of time. That's the thing about clichés. They have enough space for everyone inside, and so they can't help but make a person feel like no one at all. She looked across the table at Will, and could see him formulating an excuse. He had done it again, hadn't he? He had told. *You told,* she tried to say, but the words didn't come out. Just a short, odd sound that ended behind her tongue.

She almost knocked over the adjacent table, trying to stand up without meeting their eyes.

"Excuse you!" a kid said, scooting her chair back, laughing into her mug.

"Stephanie, come on," Will said.

She stumbled away and hoped he wouldn't follow. But the door to the café swung once and then twice without closing. That feeling of volleying an exit into someone else's hands. Will grabbed her by the elbow and led her down the block.

Outside, the sky was so beautiful, a grandiose apology.

Articulated clouds exploding into color. Stephanie felt crushed by it, and forced her eyes down. It was all in motion, she remembered, though it looked perfectly still.

"Come here. You're not thinking," Will said. "I'm only trying to help!"

"Help," Stephanie said. She wasn't sure if she was repeating what Will had said or asking for assistance.

"The guy we work for—well, I don't expect you to know. But he's a pretty big deal. It's a military contract and . . . Listen, Stephanie, I know this is personal for you, but aren't you being selfish?" he asked. "Think of the possibilities."

"This is why you were passing through town," Stephanie said. "Meetings?" She paused before: "This is why you wanted to be with me."

"Of course not," he said. But he hesitated.

People on the sidewalk were staring. What kind of details were they inventing for her life? Something to laugh about later. How had she ended up on this corner with Will—if you asked them, what would they say? Stephanie wanted to get smaller and smaller until there was nothing left of her at all. No evidence of her existence, nothing worth wondering about. No shred of information to prompt a longer story.

"Why are you here, Will?"

"Your skills dovetail with our work," he said, smiling. "We could be quite the team, the three of us. Fellowships, diplomacy, real power. Honorary degrees!"

Stephanie stopped listening somewhere around the

word *dovetail*. Offensive to the doves, long extinct. Her old friend would have thought of that. Will had been president of the bird-watching club. He had read comics in the tunnel she created in their dorm, his long legs stretched across the floor. Once, he had made her a small booklet out of scrap paper, where she could write down her feelings. She tried to remember more things, turning away. His blue T-shirt with a pun about recycling. *A glass, bottle, and can-do attitude.* The guitar she heard him play only once, sitting on the floor in the middle of the hall. A song with a predictable rhyme. Everyone could sing along. They did. The back of his head, the nape of his neck on the pillow. Lying in bed, how it felt like watching him leave her. It's a gorgeous day for a midterm, he cried. The moments before sleeping. The way he paused for other people's laughter. His dorm room, the smell of cheap candles. These candles have flavors, not scents, he'd said. She'd thought that was so funny.

Will's voice receding in the noise of everyone else's day. If you had asked a passerby, they would not have remembered Will and Stephanie ever standing there at all.

ON THE WAY home, the corner flush with garbage, the honking on the empty street. Who was alerting whom? And in the distance, a car backfiring. The other side of the road, a river along the curb that carried something filthy and glittering across its surface. A long, lean mouse running underfoot, unfazed by Stephanie. It galloped near her toes. She wondered if she was even really here. Already gone. The rodent knew she was no one.

But it was mainly the stretcher that gave her pause. That would've been the moment to consider more deeply. The tenant from the first-floor apartment was in a black bag, and the threshold of her home was taped shut. Paramedics stood on the outside steps laughing. They were watching a dance video that had received more than one million views.

Stephanie climbed the seven flights of stairs and found that her own door was open. In the kitchen, items had been moved and not returned to their rightful places. The pan of brownies in the middle of the table.

The woman from the coffee shop was nearby—her stolen coat draped over Stephanie's chair.

Stephanie backed against the wall, but something in the air lifted toward her and she stopped. There was no weapon, no visible threat. There was no one in sight, but she felt the suggestion that there had just been, that there could soon be.

It had never been her home, anyway. Not really. Where was the evidence that someone lived here, and how did they live? Who had purchased those pillows and that dish? She couldn't remember the decisions that went into the clutter on the table, the shelf. The danger tripped into guilt, and Stephanie felt a different horror, worse. A version of this moment where she had been the intruder all along.

Then on a moving train, holding the pan of brownies

in her lap. She must have left the apartment. And after that, she was standing outside a different apartment across town. Looking back, sorting through the order of events, Stephanie tried to remember the transitions, but none had been preserved. The moments stood stark against each other, never joining up, advancing toward the same conclusion, but side by side, not single file.

Edward walked toward her, emerging from the corner bistro.

"Stephanie?" he said, smiling.

"Hi," she said. She had not known where she had been heading or why. Her own intentions revealed themselves as something separate from her, approaching with the rush of oncoming traffic.

"If you come upstairs," Edward said, "I know this is silly, but I think an apology could help. Just throw it out there and see where it lands."

"Of course," Stephanie said.

"It's going to be great!" He lifted Rose in the air, and she cried with gleeful terror. "Let me go upstairs first so Annie won't smell our scheme."

She waited ten minutes before buzzing.

Hurrying down the block, a man screaming on the phone. "I don't have to deal with this!" he said.

In a high window, someone listening to an old song through crappy speakers. No, it was a new version of an old song. The speakers made it sound closer to the past.

She could have walked away. Those ten minutes could have gone differently. Stephanie did things differently so many times in her mind that she started to believe she had changed the incident, remembered it wrong. She had done things right in retrospect. But that didn't count.

"Can I come in?" Stephanie said.

"Of course," Annie said. Her face fell—and then, the way her smile concealed another expression. Maybe if Annie had not been so abrupt, if she had not bared her teeth. If she had not squinted at the pan of brownies or given Edward a sideways glance. Maybe then Stephanie would have taken more care.

Stephanie, Annie, and Edward on the terrace once again. Her terrace, their terrace, it did not matter. She apologized, and Annie rolled her eyes. She was not holding the brownies anymore, she was holding Rose, and the baby squirmed and reached, crawling over Stephanie's legs. Annie lifted Rose away, and Stephanie observed them together, mother and daughter. She felt a sort of closure, but not closure with Annie and her family. Closure with the world. She was not welcome here. She could not go back to her building or back to Will. She could not go anywhere at all. A new kind of loneliness; it was absolute. It cratered every other impulse. She wondered what it would take to leave this place forever. She did not know how to do it, but then her body did.

Stephanie's body, blocking the door.

Annie, safe in the kitchen, washing up at the sink.

Reflected in the doorknob, Stephanie could see Edward and Rose behind her, still on the terrace, their figures round and small, her body foregrounding the scene. They were all contained in a little brass bubble.

A passing thought: would ending her life also end theirs? Stephanie was not sure.

She was about to do something terrible. Always, she had assumed she was misunderstood, but that's because she had thought events happened in order. She had not yet met the worst version of herself, the one everyone else had anticipated. Now the grammar of her life was finally in agreement, and her stomach unclenched. Her heart was pounding. She had watched Edward and Annie invent their Terrace Stories, lies to populate the outdoor space. Stephanie would do the reverse. She would take something she had considered false about herself and here, on the terrace, she would make it true. Even if she could have changed her mind, her body had already decided it was too late.

Stephanie clicked the terrace door shut.

The birdsong, the sound of the wind gathering and rushing up to fill some invisible container. The edge of Annie's scream making its way over the vanishing threshold. For once, nothing was blurred. Everything was crisp and precise, the deliberate lines of a decision that cannot be rewound. The terrace heightened and stretched into a searing single line. Stephanie felt a pulling, a pain that covered her entire person. She felt the presence of Edward and Rose too. Her body pulling apart, then plummeting back together, with the kind of finality only present in moments of disaster.

LATER, STEPHANIE THOUGHT about the rings on the tree trunks behind the Madisons' house. She had added rings where there were none. That wasn't making space—that was making something else.

SHE FELL TO her knees and did not stand until Eddie's hands came up under her arms, brought her to her feet.

On one side of the terrace door, Annie existed. But when they opened the door again, Annie did not exist. There was no Annie anymore. Annie was in her old kitchen, dumbstruck, looking for her family. Stephanie knew it instantly, probably because she had done the math, the sad geometry of extracting this family and placing them somewhere else. Sometime else. The shock of entering their empty apartment, where Annie did not exist, of being somewhere and then ending up nowhere at all. The sharp smell of acetone entered Stephanie's nostrils and stung, making her eyes water.

"Hey, are you okay?" Eddie asked from the room in Stephanie's mind. But no—he was here, standing beside her. It was as if the room and reality had switched places, and she realized their old life, the one they had so recently known, was now only available in dreams.

There were small differences on the other side of the door. A tangent world. Crows had not yet gone extinct, but most other birds had. Bigger changes too. The seasons had fractured into splinters too small to consider. Airplanes, something from history books. Everything was moving faster here toward its conclusion. An ending can accelerate the events in its circumference.

Eddie thought his wife had abandoned him, abandoned Rosie. For a few days at least. He had Stephanie join them for dinner. She was the only one who understood, anyway. He cried openly and she tried to comfort him.

"She'll come back, right?" Eddie asked, sobbing.

"I'm sure she'll come back," Stephanie lied. There was no Annie on this side of the door.

"What did I do wrong?" Eddie asked. Stephanie did not answer. She put a trembling hand on his arm.

But why wasn't Annie picking up her phone? he wanted to know. Why was the number disconnected?

Stephanie almost tried to explain.

Then one night, Eddie broke down and told her the story of the terrace, told Stephanie about her own special power, as if she had not spent every day in the unfolding calamity of empty and expanding space. It was like listening to a lullaby about her life, but sung by someone three towns over.

"We should've explained," he said, begging her forgiveness. "We took advantage. We should've said something. It's all my fault."

She watched him wear an apron and make pasta wheels for Rosie. She watched the changes dawn on him. The slow burgeoning fact of Stephanie. Her lack of surprise. Her lack of proper despair. The discomfort. How his manner shifted. She felt immense pain for this person pulled into the circumference of her ending.

He put Rosie in her crib, then turned to Stephanie in the dark.

"What have you done?" he asked her. "Where are we?"

"I don't know," she said. "I don't know."

On the other side of the door, there was no Doris, no popular memoir titled *Darlings,* with its quotable first line, "It was the fucking worst of times." The books that Stephanie remembered, so many missing. There was no boy from calculus. There was no Stephanie, taking on new clients, stealing them from Annie. She watched their old boss in the old parking lot, fumbling for the keys to a different car. No one to take under her wing. She looked so desperate, standing there, carrying too many bags. Stephanie had never considered that her own presence might have made someone else feel less alone.

There was a Grand Canyon but no Mall of America. Mount Rushmore was there, but Stephanie only recognized three of the four faces.

Eddie allowed her to hang around. The isolation was too much for him to bear.

"I don't want you here," he said, "but I don't want you to leave."

They knew something no one else knew. Stephanie loitered in his kitchen, sat silently next to Rosie at the dinner table, passing her peanut butter puffs and juice. She did not dare speak unless spoken to. She wondered, if she tried to say the right words, would they be new words? Would she even know what they meant?

She fell asleep on his couch one night and woke up

to Eddie holding her, making small sounds against her shoulder. Stephanie cried then too, and they held each other, crying.

"I'm sorry," she said.

"Don't," he said, "bother."

They tried to do more. Eddie eased down her pants and she ran her hands over his shoulders, under his shirt. They did not make a sound. They drifted deeper into each other's arms, but it wasn't right. Eddie pulled away, covering his face. That was the last time Stephanie allowed herself to be part of their family. She put on her shoes and he walked her downstairs, let her out onto the street. Different markings on the pavement, different rules for alternate-side parking.

No more Eddie and Rosie. Alone. Stephanie disappeared into herself. She could not imagine a better place to get lost. Of course, there were moments of weakness. Watching father and daughter during their Sunday routine from afar, following them through a farmers' market. (What is that purple vegetable? Other side of the door.) Under the pedestrian bridge, around the park fountain that stayed dry through every season. Eventually, she gave up keeping track. Wedges of doorstopping silver light arrived at her window each night, a different kind of evening glow than anything Stephanie could remember from before. And the rain here, the sound against the roof, slightly tinnier, mean and prehistoric.

It took her a while to figure out how to ask for the things she wanted. Everything seemed difficult to obtain.

Usually, she settled for something nearly right. There were strange thoughts that traveled across her mind. Ideas chaperoned by other, unfamiliar ideas. Sometimes a feeling would knock her sideways, and no matter how she tried, she could not find its name. Loneliness was there, sharp, serrated. Joy rarely arrived. An oval paperweight with bubbles under the glass, always approaching the surface, never rising to the top.

Stephanie resolved to end her life. If, for instance, a crevice appeared between the floor of the apartment and the ceiling below her, she could stay there forever, starve, freeze, sleep. But when she tried to press the crevice through that well-worn angle in her mind, nothing happened. She tried something simpler, enlarging a box of crackers, but still, everything remained the same.

Later that night, she looked at the crackers, and the box shrank to half its size.

"Oh," Stephanie said.

She wanted to die, but here, on the other side of the door, she could only make things smaller. The desire to die remained small too. She could not make enough room for the idea to grow into action, and so the impulse to do something about it hardened, calcified, stayed. Just a permanent fixture in Stephanie's mind that, after a time, had more to do with living than to do with death. The feeling remained, and so did she.

Maybe Will and his friends had been right. You can't have addition without subtraction. Maybe all these years she had been borrowing from the other side of the door.

IF YOU HAD asked someone about Stephanie around this time, they would have said, who's Stephanie? Aren't you paying attention? Everything is endangered. Everything is gone. The science teacher who used to play lacrosse, also on this side of the door. "What's the matter?" he asked his classes, every September. Because his students often cried.

But Stephanie—she was a very hard worker, people might have said, if pressed. That's because most of the people who knew her were people from work. Smart. Beige. Punctual, quiet. A waste of time, maybe, one boss would have said. She's not from around here, another employer would have noted. Or no: She's not from anywhere. This was the employer in the building where Stephanie ended up doing secretarial work for the next ten years. No one ever had a problem with her, but no one ever had a laugh with her either. She made her cubicle an inch or two smaller. Safe, cramped, tiny. She was a wisp of a person at the periphery of plot, rarely drifting into anyone's dreams or desires.

She met the occasional man. He'd notice her, drawn to her way of moving through the world. Extraterrestrial, he'd think. Outta sight, he'd think. Fucking was like entering another state of consciousness. She'd somehow get smaller underneath him—did she actually disappear?—and he would shudder, despite himself, coughing, how embarrassing. And then after, sitting next to her, the profound sadness. An unholy feeling, something amiss. Missing a place that did not exist. Scouring for a location on a map. No longitude or latitude. A sour pit in his stomach. He would leave her in the middle of the night. Would not return her calls. And much later, at a bar, he'd have a little too much to drink. He'd tell the bartender the story of his erstwhile affair and come upon this sentence, which would give him great satisfaction, since he could so rarely find the right words for the things that had happened to him, but these words arrived as if by design on the brim of his story:

"Once you visit the country of Stephanie, you never leave."

At the other end of the bar, Eddie was having a drink after a long day of work. Rosie was with the sitter. Sometimes he listened to people talk. This was his strength on the other side of the door, disappearing just long enough to hear the truth. He overheard what the man said, bristling at the sound of her name. But there are a lot of Stephanies in this world, Eddie thought. In both worlds, the world from before too. Eddie liked to think he was generous in this way, understanding that the world did not revolve around him, even when he felt like maybe it did. It could have been another Stephanie. It could have happened to anyone, he thought when he missed his wife. Anyone at all.

STEPHANIE HAD A pain in her lower back that only got worse. After a few months, someone on the janitorial staff in the office noticed her early in the morning, hunched at her desk, wincing.

"Here," the janitor said, handing her a slip of paper with the name and address of a free clinic.

Stephanie took the afternoon off from work the next day and went to the doctor.

"I don't want to scare you," the doctor said, "but I've never seen anything like it."

"What's wrong with me?" she asked.

"Your organs. Like an accordion. Like they've been stretched."

He referred her to a specialist, who invited her to be part of a medical study. There were two other cases like hers; he found the patients and the physicians online and thought maybe they could compare notes, start fundraising. A new disease needs a new nonprofit.

A window in the specialist's office looked out across an alley and onto another window. The windows peered directly into each other, like lovers. This was the type of hidden place that Stephanie used to crave. In the opposite window, a cat paced the sill, then tucked itself against the glass. Was it her family's cat, from all those years ago? To Stephanie, it was just a shadow of something nearly saved, then lost.

"So, what do you think?" the specialist asked her.

Stephanie said no.

She walked to her apartment and gently eased herself down onto the couch, fell asleep facing the wall. The late afternoon light danced against the paint. When she opened her eyes again, the light was still dancing, but it was a new light. A new day had started.

Maybe it was because of the horrible ache. She was tired and sore. Maybe it was just the right time. She had been away for so long. That morning Stephanie packed a bag and drove home.

BACK ON THE other side of the door, Annie mourned the loss of her family. Presidents were elected—yes, the ones you remember. The Madison girl sold Stephanie's parents' house. Stephanie's parents took their life savings and moved to a retirement community and played golf, bridge, canasta. When people asked if they had children, they did not mention their daughters. They said it had been an easy choice. Why bother with kids when their lives had been so full? Just the two of them. More than enough. They sat at the pool on Thursdays with their book club, and on the first Tuesday of every month they hosted a potluck dinner.

Deep at the bottom of a drawer, her mother still had a picture of the four of them, together.

ON STEPHANIE'S SIDE of the door, the boy from calculus never married the Madison girl because he had never existed. The Madison girl (here she was named Beth, there she had been Lucy) never went into real estate, never called anything a "charming feature," never sold Stephanie's parents' house. When Stephanie walked up to the old porch, she could see them inside, her mother and father, standing around a familiar countertop. The wallpaper was the same and so was the second-floor bedroom, with its slightly higher ceiling. The stars are brighter in the suburbs, she thought, looking up at the sky, then watching her family through the window.

Her parents were laughing, eating some sort of dip. Standing between them was a woman in her late twenties holding a blue bowl of chips, big cheeks, giggling silently. The young woman saw Stephanie first, and how she recognized her, no one really knows. She dropped the bowl on the ground and ran to the front door.

IF YOU HAD asked someone about Stephanie around this time, they would've said, It's just the most curious thing. Her appearing like this, after all these years. After she died that day by the playground. The accident. Horrible! Is it a ghost? Is it even Stephanie? they'd ask among themselves. Does it really matter? other people replied. Who cares if it's the real Stephanie or not? Hasn't that poor family been through enough?

But of course, it was Stephanie. Stephanie from the other side of the door. She remembered things that no one else remembered. Her mother wearing sunglasses inside. The opaque cup. The distaste for peppers. The waffles, the babysitter. The glow-in-the-dark stars, long since painted over.

The sisters spent time together, but Stephanie needed a lot of sleep, now that it was close to the end. Her parents hired a hospice nurse to treat the pain, and he came once a day with a medication that made Stephanie fuzzy. The hours were smudged collages done by a child, and she was not sure which parts were real. One picture, her little sister sitting next to the bed telling Stephanie about graduate school. Another, her mother massaging her feet. A cold washcloth on her forehead. Her father in the doorway: Does she need a glass of water? Do we have to watch her die again?

All the people and things lost on the other side of the door. But they were not lost completely. They existed here too, because Stephanie remembered them. She had made room for them in her story. The lakes, the paperbacks from her high shelf, the flute solo played poorly at a party, late at night. Will—a favorite scene from a movie that she had transposed into the plot of a different film altogether.

Stephanie's little sister started a lot of sentences this way: "If you hadn't walked out into the street that day." The second half of the sentence was always different: Things would have been more normal. Mom would not have lost all that weight. Dad would not have had to develop a sense of humor. The town would not have renovated the park. I would have had a sister.

But you had me all along, Stephanie said, maybe out loud, maybe not. Her eyes were closed, yet she still had enough strength to reduce the space, make the distance between her and her sister a little bit smaller. They were holding hands. She could make their minds meet. Silently,

Stephanie told the story of living all this time on the other side of the world. Now the distance was not so distant. Her sister was near. Nearest and dearest—yes, precisely. Come find me, she said. You're almost here. We're so close. We're almost one and the same.

CANTILEVER

AT THE SPACE STATION, ROSIE WAS KNOWN AS GRAVITY ONE.
She operated the small vestibule on the tip of the hub
that kept the suburb in orbit. All around Gravity One,
concentric circles of tiny single-person homes, like a sleek
Levittown in the sky.

When Rosie took on extra shifts, she worked with
the relocation department down in the atrium. She inter-
viewed potential homesteaders who had made the long
journey to their suburb, hoping for a chance at life in the
nebula. It was interesting work, and it paid the bills, which
was more than you could say for some jobs. Rosie didn't
mind hearing people's stories from the planet. It made her
feel closer to something that was nearly gone.

One weekend, an older woman knocked on Rosie's
cube. Rosie was done with the day's work and looking
forward to a drink with her friends. Her girlfriend, Kyle,
was traveling to a distant suburb that had ruptured and
needed to be restrung. She called Rosie when she could,
but the reception was not great.

"Dear Rosie: No matter how many moons we colo-
nize, we will never make a decent cell phone," Kyle said
in a message to comms. The office brought Rosie a vel-
lum printout of Kyle's note, which she then tacked above

her desk. It was like an old-fashioned love letter, Todd remarked, looking over Rosie's shoulder on his way to lunch.

Kyle always knew how to make Rosie laugh. They were saving money to buy a place closer to the atmosphere. The mortgages were cheaper, but not all the areas were toxic like people said. And you could fit more heads in each homestead; they could give shelter to some of their friends, that was allowed. Kyle was always taking care of people. Rosie loved her but had not yet said the words.

"Hello?" The older woman peered around Rosie's door, and Rosie sighed.

"Hi there," she said. "Do you have an appointment?"

"Oh, I don't think so."

"You need an appointment to start the interview process," Rosie explained. "They can set you up outside the atrium."

The woman looked confused, startled. She stared at Rosie. Maybe she was unwell. A lot of people had a rough time with the initial journey. Rosie softened.

"Are you okay?" she asked, bringing a chair closer so the woman could sit down.

"I'm fine, I'm fine, just a little tired."

"What's your name? I'm Rosie."

"That was my grandmother's name. Rose."

"No kidding," Rosie said. "My dad is the only one who calls me that. Rose. Here, let me get you some juice."

Rosie spun her chair around to the other side of the cube and dispensed some orange drink into a paper cup.

"Rosie, see, I have an appointment, but with someone else."

"With Todd?" Rosie asked.

"Yes, that's the one," the woman said. "I met with Todd but asked if I could meet with you instead."

Rosie laughed. "Well, that's not typically allowed, but as someone who knows Todd, I feel your pain."

"Would you . . ." The woman took a deep gulp of the orange drink and swallowed. "Ah, much better. Rose, would you be willing to do my interview? I know it's the end of the day. You must have so many friends. So many places to be. But I've come so far, and I've waited so long to meet you."

Rosie felt a familiar undertow. The woman was frail and would probably not make it through to the final round. She could message Sharon and Easy and ask them to save her a seat at the bar.

"You know what?" she said. "It's your lucky day. I've just had my last session and would be happy to do your intake."

The older woman smiled. "Thank you. You're not breaking any rules for me, are you?"

"Only the silly ones," Rosie said.

BEFORE ROSIE MET Kyle at orientation, she noticed her standing on the tiny balcony between floors with a few friends, eating the boxed lunches. It felt important that Rosie had to look up to see her for the first time. *Heads up,* her dad used to say when Rosie would daydream on the couch, which was always.

Kyle sang louder than anyone else in their cohort, louder even than Sharon, a voluminous off-key soprano. Kyle did not like space seafood because it gave her cramps. Kyle had a jacket with patches on both arms. Then Rosie started thinking about all the things she didn't know. She called these the Questions, and they hovered about her with benevolent persistence. How did Kyle look when she brushed her teeth? How did she look when she was sorry? Did she sleep on her back or on her side, with her arm curled under the standard-issue pillows? What bored her, what inspired her? Where did she like to be touched? All the comings and goings of a person before they meet you. Meeting a new person is a constant suspension of disbelief, Rosie thought, because they are always expanding, illogically, alarmingly, endlessly. Night after night, staring at the bunk above her, she tried to guess the answers. She wanted to know the situation of Kyle's life, even if the full story remained hidden forever.

Then their training was over, and Kyle and Rosie were the last recruits left at the end of the annual Spyglass Party. Kyle leaned her whole body forward. *What now, Rosie?* she seemed to say. Rosie felt an effervescence in her chest and wondered how many times you have to imagine something before it becomes real. The softness of Kyle's mouth. It was already happening! She had nearly missed it, on account of anticipation. Kyle took Rosie's face in her hands.

Once, Rosie knew, you could pay to see a show in a theater, on a stage, and something called a spotlight would direct your gaze, tell you the parts of the story that were important, like a finger touching the base of your chin and lifting your eyes toward the most crucial detail. At the Spyglass Party they stayed talking until the early morning, sitting in a single girder of light, and whether the glow was artificial or lunar, neither Rosie nor Kyle could tell.

"LET'S BEGIN," ROSIE said, unloading a stack of forms on her desk, opening her screen to the survey pages. "I have to do the boring part first, please forgive me."

"I'm not bored," the woman said, smiling, her cheeks growing large. Some of the color had been restored to her face, but she was watching Rosie in a way that made her wonder if the woman might not still feel faint or need resuscitation.

"Oh, just you wait. I promise I won't disappoint. Now, this is the part where I tell you that your odds are not good."

"I know that already."

"Okay. I still have to say it. Only three percent of applicants are admitted to the suburbs, and most of those applicants are in good physical shape, of sound mind, and, um. Wealthy."

"I heard that it was only one percent," the woman said. This was true. Rosie had lied. But it was part of her job to lie, and part of her job to continue the lie, even though the woman was right.

"Don't believe everything you hear!" Rosie said.

"Well then!" the woman said. "How could I be bored? You're telling me something brand-new."

"It says here that you've already done your physical. I don't have those results, and I won't see them. This is more of a psychological intake."

"You're gonna shrink me, eh?"

"No. Not psychological exactly. Biographical? Historical."

"Okay," the woman said. Her eyes were wide. She hung on Rosie's every word.

"Think of the suburbs as time capsules. We are trying to create the most intricate time capsules possible. The best stories. The most useful knowledge. The information."

"What about love?" the woman asked.

Rosie was confused. "What do you mean?"

"Are you also collecting love, or just information?"

"Well, these are solo homesteads, so you won't be with anyone. It will just be you, alone. You can visit the hub, of course. But other than that."

"I see," the woman said. She looked over the top of Rosie's head, her eyes investigating something so far out of view that it had probably happened in the past.

"Did you know all of this before coming here?" Rosie asked, concerned. The homestead advertising was very clear about the available space, the limits, the rationale for keeping people apart. These were the elderly who would not procreate, who would die first.

"Of course, I know the details. I just reject your premise," the woman said.

"What premise?"

"The premise that there is no love when a person is alone."

ROSIE AND KYLE finished training and were assigned to their posts. Gravity One and Repair Circuit Four. These were good jobs, the best they could hope for. The really good jobs, the great jobs, were set aside for sons of senators, diplomats, people with honorary degrees. Kyle and Rosie were the only daughters of single parents. It was amazing they had come this far. When they had said goodbye to their fathers, they knew that they would not see them again. Of course, they had tried to find a loophole to navigate, a string to pull for their families. But there were no strings to pull. The strings did not exist.

They marked the occasion with modest farewell parties. Tablecloths were produced, still retaining the ringed impressions of old glassware, vintage folds from their years in storage. Hoarded bottles of champagne idled on windowsills into the morning, their shallow dregs flattening with the procession of time. In the residence cube, their bodies tangled together, Rosie and Kyle reminisced about how the party had moved into the backyard because the air had been good that night. How Rosie had made everyone sit in a circle on the ground because there hadn't been enough chairs. How the neighbor had complained about the noise but then had joined the gathering himself, had even given Kyle a gift, for what was there left to celebrate anymore? What was there left to complain about? Much later, Rosie found it hard to remember if their parties were two separate events or if they had celebrated that night together.

Rosie's father helped her pack the bags provided by suburb staffing. Small, lithe duffels that could be carried on any part of the body with a swift adjustment of straps. Rosie moved to zip the bags herself but found that she wanted him to do it.

"Can you?"

He looked so relieved that she had asked.

"I will see you in my dreams," he said. She did not know if he saw her, but she saw him. He was usually making toast in the kitchen, but the kitchen was much too far away. Then he sat down in his weekend clothes and told her about his day, still on the other side of the room, retreating fast into the dark.

"WHEN YOU THINK about your childhood, what are the key points of interest?" Rosie asked.

"I was raised by my grandmother," the woman said.

"Rose?"

"Yes, exactly. My parents died when I was young. My mother wrote about extinction."

"Was she a scholar? I have a box here that I can check for scholars and inventors. That could be helpful."

"No, she wrote articles, and a book. Does that count? That word would have made her laugh," the woman said. "*Scholar.*"

"Okay, I'll put *writer*. And your father?"

"He was a historian."

"I can write *scholar* for him," Rosie offered.

"Sure. He was an academic. We had a beautiful home. But it was falling apart. There was a crumbling stone structure in the backyard where I used to play games."

"Was it an archaeological site, or a landmark?"

"No, nothing like that. Just a pile of rocks really. It was like a little satellite orbiting our house."

"I see," Rosie said.

"There were ghost stories of course. Does that count?"

"No, sorry. Only real things."

The woman looked at Rosie with an expression that resembled pity. Was she disappointed? Rosie felt reprimanded, as though she had not met some secret measure of character. But she did not know the metrics or where she had fallen short.

"And then after that you lived with your grandmother?" she asked.

"Yes."

Rosie made some notes and swiped through several screens on her monitor.

"Okay, here's one of the trippy questions."

"Trippy?" the woman asked.

"Yeah," Rosie said, laughing. "That's not the official term, it's just what I call them. There are three questions during intake that are . . . a little far-out."

"I'm ready," the woman said, taking another sip of the orange drink and putting the cup down on the floor by her feet. She was wearing shabby loafers, the sight of which moved Rosie. No one wore loafers in space.

"Here it goes: Can you tell me about one remarkable smell from your life?"

"Your hair," the woman said without taking a beat to think.

Rosie grabbed her curls instinctively. "Oh no. What's wrong with it?"

"No, I didn't mean . . ."

"It always looks like shit by the end of the day. Sorry! Sorry, language."

"There's nothing wrong with it, nothing at all. I was just noticing. I like it pulled back like that."

"Oh," Rosie said, suddenly embarrassed. "My girl-friend likes it when I wear it like this. I think it makes my ears look big."

The woman laughed. "It's very pretty. Can you ask the question again, Rose?"

"Sure. Tell me about one remarkable smell from your life."

"Well, probably the smell after alighting. Like nail pol-ish remover."

Rosie was surprised. "You alighted?"

"Yes. I paid someone."

"It's illegal," Rosie said.

The woman smiled.

"Look, I hate to do this, but I'm going to have to put that on a separate red form."

"I know."

"It's for security reasons. But also, for your own health and safety."

"I know. That's fine. You should do your job."

"I'm sorry," Rosie said.

"Don't apologize."

Rosie jotted down the violation code in brackets, then ticked the necessary boxes. She was shaking her head, impressed. The woman was from a different time step. Even the rumored acetone smell was real. People speculated it was because of memory, how the most important smells could not travel with you, the sharp, sterile odor replacing everything from before.

Maybe Rosie could ask her things about her world on the other side. But that might be rude, and dangerous. Sharon and Easy would lose their minds over this. Kyle would lose her mind too. She wished there were some way to call Kyle, to tell her right now. If only the intake process weren't confidential. If only Kyle weren't so far away.

"Can I ask why you did it? Your alightment," Rosie asked.

"I was separated from my family," the woman said. "A long time ago."

"And did you find them here, on the other side?" Rosie

asked. Now she was the one hanging on the woman's every word.

The woman smiled and looked away.

"Yes."

THE FIRST TIME Rosie heard about it was on the television program, like everyone else. The woman who claimed her sister had moved through the corridor of time. Rosie's dad was shimming the leg of their dining table, but he stopped moving when the news anchor started talking, and he didn't move for a long time after that. He just sat there, suspended, holding the leg of the table like the whole world would topple if he let go. Rosie was coloring in her book, but she had finished coloring inside the lines. She went back and colored outside the lines too. Why waste all that blank space, Rosie thought. Deep into the night, her dad was still sitting on the floor with his toolbox, and Rosie helped herself to cereal before bed.

It wasn't until later that they had a word for it, *alightment,* and the word made it sound like it had always existed, solid and sure and believed, a shim under a wobbly leg. The knowing of the word became a substitute for actual knowledge, because no one really knew how it felt, what it sounded like, where it lived in your mind after it happened. At Rosie's school, near the monkey bars, the kids played house. But on the swing set, past the old cafeteria and the sunken classrooms, they played time. They acted out a version of what it would look like and how it would be. You push the swing, and I will ride the swing to the other side. Rosie and her friends launched from the swings midflight, landing with a velocity that took their feet into an involuntary sprint. Then they were spinning and falling, until they were all on the ground, laughing, having forgotten the original premise. This was Rosie's favorite kind of game, the kind that becomes something new halfway through playing.

Most people didn't survive the process. Most people did not know how to alight, or how to pay someone. Most people had never met someone from a different time step. Of course, there were days when Rosie felt out of step with her world, a little out of sorts. Not belonging, not from anywhere at all. But Kyle always said, "Welcome, hello, we saved you a seat, it's called being a person."

"Do you want to take a break?" Rosie asked.

The woman shook her head. She swiveled around once in her chair, staring up at the ceiling through Rosie's cube. Rosie had not looked up in ages, but now she did, curious to see if the woman's regard had maybe changed the view. It was a skylight in the grandest sense, cosmic flight, debris, the asteroid belt, and in the distance, the suburb proper, concentric rings orbiting Rosie's vestibule. THE STARS ARE BRIGHTER IN THE SUBURBS! the billboards read, plastered across what remained of the planet. The advertisements had the consonance of truth, but no, the stars were not necessarily brighter here. The homesteads were just closer to the source of the light. Rosie could not decide if this made the signs untrue or if it made the signs more beautiful for their nearness to the truth, their failure to fully arrive. No one knew how to say exactly what they meant. Kyle would tuck her hand in Rosie's waistband and just rest it there against her skin. And Rosie would reach for the words adjacent to the words that were important.

"That's where I normally work," Rosie said, directing the woman's gaze to the center of the suburb.

"That tiny dot?" the woman asked.

"That's me. Gravity One." The woman looked at her, confused, and Rosie laughed. "It's just a job title, but people sort of use it as a name."

"It's a good proper noun," the woman said, marveling. "Gravity One. So austere and important."

"It sounds more important than it is, truly," Rosie said. "It's basically a menial job."

The woman didn't respond. Maybe she was waiting for Rosie to share more? She looked at her with an expression Rosie didn't recognize. Maybe she was feeling an emotion from the other side. Rosie laughed again, a nervous habit.

"We should probably move on," the woman said, as if she had read Rosie's mind.

"Yes! Yes. This part is simple. This part is about employment."

"Well, I worked in sales for thirty years."

"Okay. So, anything you can give me that might turn

a head or raise an eyebrow. Anything interesting. For instance, what did you sell?" Rosie asked.

"It's the funniest thing," the woman said. "You won't believe me. But I don't even remember."

"Was it stocks, or bonds, or maybe real estate?"

"No, nothing like that."

"Did you sell . . . let's see . . . oil, coal, linoleum, weapons, or another natural resource?"

The woman laughed. "Thank you for trying. As you'll soon find out, I'm a very boring old lady who has led an unremarkable life."

"Oh no, don't say that. These questions are . . . . Well, they're bogus."

"Bogus, eh?"

"What I mean is, I'm sure your life has been remarkable." Rosie looked down at the red form. "Unfortunately, I can't ask you about your family, since it falls under the category of your alightment."

"That's no problem," the woman said.

"Sales," Rosie repeated, swiping through to a new screen. "Did you sell . . . people?"

"No," the woman said. "No, no, I didn't sell people."

"I'm sorry. It's one of the questions."

The woman looked back up through the skylight and peered around Rosie's work space.

"It might've had to do with . . . ," she started, but abruptly stopped talking and stared at the ground. "No, never mind. It's gone." The woman's eyes filled with something like frustration, but emptier. Rosie wanted to tell her it was fine, not to worry. She didn't know how. It wasn't nearly fine at all. The woman paced over to the drink dispenser and filled her cup until it was orange to the brim.

On Kyle's first repair trip, she was out of signal for a month. Rosie tried to stay positive, but mostly she just thought about the end of the world, which would likely happen in their lifetime. They were so lucky to have been sent off planet, and now her girlfriend was going to die on a trip to a distant suburb held in artificial orbit around a distant space station, manned by a distant stranger, someone just like Rosie, someone named Gravity Twelve.

"It all seems so pointless," Rosie said to Sharon at the hub. "Why even bother caring about someone if they could just vanish one day?"

"Why can't you worry about cheating like a normal person?" Sharon asked. "I've heard Gravity Twelve is a total fox."

"With all due respect, foxes have been extinct for decades."

"Exactly! It would be priceless if your girlfriend left you for a totally extinct fox."

"I know where the mole is on Kyle's big toe. What am I supposed to do with that information?" Rosie asked.

Sharon hugged her then, and Easy joined them later with distracting stories from comms. They had too much to drink and went on the homestead listing service, a favorite pastime, picking out the houses where they would live near the atmosphere, together. There was one property with a nimbus view. An Orion split-level with an office space. The Cassiopeia condos.

At the end of the night Kyle sent a message. She was on her way back.

"HERE'S TRIPPY QUESTION number two," Rosie said.

"I'm tripping over all of them, but go ahead."

"I will show you a picture, and you tell me one thing you see." Rosie shuffled through a box of large, laminated images and held up her favorite print. A king and a queen sitting together in an enchanted forest. There were lots of things to pick up on in the facsimile of the painting. The thrones, the crowns, the jewels. There was the hermit in the corner under the eaves. Most people saw that first. Then the other hermits hidden in the . . . Rosie did not know the word. Well, their faces were deep between the branches, set back into the brushstrokes. There were all sorts of extinct creatures, and Rosie expected that the woman might see some of those first, what with her mother's specialty in extinction. Something called a rabbit lingered at the front of the scene, but if you weren't paying attention, it looked like just another fold in the queen's robes.

The woman leaned in close and took her time. She put on a pair of glasses that had been tucked away in the neck of her shirt and studied the painting carefully.

"Do I tell you everything I see, or just one thing?" the woman asked.

"Just one thing."

"That's easy. A family," the woman said.

Rosie was surprised. That word wasn't on her list, so she had to open a separate tab on the monitor, add a new box, and copy the answer over to the form.

"Did I say something wrong?" the woman asked.

"No, it's just that." Rosie turned over her shoulder. "Well, applicants don't usually see two people and think of families."

"Why not?"

It was a fair question. Rosie didn't know. She thought of her own two-person family. Her dad, still making breakfast in some hidden kitchen that only materialized on the hinge of her dreams.

"Anyway, there aren't two people in the painting," the woman said. "There's nearly a dozen. And then the plants and the animals, and farther away, you can see even more. It stretches out forever. A family."

Then Rosie remembered Kyle's idea for their homestead. Anyone and everyone they could fit would be welcome. They would put a bed under the sink, Kyle had teased, right next to their jar of shiny tokens. Why hadn't there been a message yet? It had been so many weeks. Rosie started to cry.

"Oh no," the woman said. "Now I'm definitely not part of that three percent."

"It's nothing. It's not you. I'm so sorry!" Rosie covered her face in shame. She couldn't afford to lose these extra shifts.

"Don't apologize," the woman said, slipping a handkerchief into Rosie's palm. It smelled like . . . Well, there wasn't a word for what it smelled like, at least not a word that Rosie knew. It was a specific ingredient in a type of detergent the woman used, long ago, when she did the wash. But if Rosie could have named it, she would have listed it on her intake form as the most remarkable smell from her lifetime. The same smell that was nestled in the folds of her father's favorite old shirt.

"Thank you, you're so kind," Rosie said, wiping her cheeks and her nose, pressing the soft linen under each of her eyes. "I just haven't heard. My girlfriend, she's on a long journey."

"I'm so sorry. You must be worried."

"I am."

"We can just sit here if you want. We don't have to do the intake forms."

Rosie looked up at her. The woman was stroking her back lightly and smiling, waiting patiently.

"I didn't realize that I was so upset," Rosie said.

"That's all right. You don't have to know everything. It's okay to be surprised."

Rosie motioned to give the handkerchief back to the woman, but the woman shook her head.

"No, that's for you."

THE PERSON WHO invented the suburbs had already died.
That's how quickly time was moving now. If you blinked,
you missed an entire story. And stories seemed to stop
before they'd even started, supported only at one end by
the teller, then wobbled out carefully like a beam into the
unknown. It did not make sense to keep track of things
when they did not know whom they were keeping track
for. They did it anyway. All Rosie wanted was a person
on the other end of her stories. She would receive their
stories and they would receive hers. "What a time to be
alive," Kyle would say, grabbing Rosie around her middle
and lifting her in the air.

The future and the past were on either side of a bridge,
and no matter which way Rosie walked, the sun was in
her eyes.

ROSIE CAUGHT HER breath while the woman signed vari-
ous waivers, stuck her thumbs in blue ink, and pressed
the fingers to a plastic slide. She watched the woman scan
the text carefully, reading every form with her pinky as a
pointer, then shuffling the pages to the back of the file
and starting a new document. Under the desk was a map
of the suburbs, the luminescent flotsam and the giant un-
knowns, blank space sprawling across the borders of the
blueprint. And under that, plans for new suburbs extending as far as the imagination could witness.

"Let's finish out the interview before it gets too late,"
Rosie said.

"Are you sure?" the woman asked. "We can stop. You can just submit whatever you have."

"No, that's not fair to you. There's only one question left. And who knows? Maybe you'll be in the lucky three percent."

"Who knows?" The woman smiled, rolling in her chair, back and away to the other side of the room.

Rosie composed herself and swiped through to the final screen. She dried her eyes once more on the side of her sleeve. "Here's the last question, and then we'll get you sent down to the bunks and shower stations."

"I'm ready."

"How much money is left in your planet bank account?"

The woman looked alarmed. "That isn't the last question."

"It is," Rosie said.

"What about the third trippy question?"

"This is it," Rosie said.

The woman exhaled and put her hands on her thighs. "Twenty-three. Twenty-three dollars."

"Okay. You're all set."

Rosie closed the file and sent it through a pneumatic tube, like the ones they used to have at the drive-through pharmacy. The woman awkwardly hovered in the corner, waiting for further instructions. Rosie looked at her again. Maybe she was feeling vulnerable about Kyle, or maybe it was something else unseen. A story cantilevered out into her hands from a starry messenger, and Rosie knew she was meant to receive it, even if the contents and origin were unclear.

"Do you want to have dinner with me?" Rosie asked. "I'm off for the rest of the night."

The woman smiled.

Rosie told Sharon and Easy that they should go on without her. She took the woman to the main dining pavilion in the atrium.

"The food is terrible, but the views," Rosie said.

THEY SAT ACROSS from each other in one of the booths that looked out on a construction ship. The woman remembered a good day with her baby and her husband at a shack on a pier. Boats docked and fresh fish sandwiches for sale. And another time, earlier, when she was not much more than a baby herself. Her parents sandwiching her on a bench near some sailboats, eating fries. The grease from the fries turning the paper cone translucent. The way the boats sat patiently waiting in the water, even though her family did not rent a boat, not in the first memory or the second. They just wanted to be near the boats, to feel like later they could. Maybe they would.

This was sort of like that, but shinier. The metallic gleam of space. The construction ship drifted at an angle that made the woman dizzy. She could not decide if it was saner, these unforgiving surfaces, or just a different and mellower sort of distress. The loneliness of the landscape landed on her heart with a curious, cold thrum.

The woman swirled her food product but did not eat anything. Nothing tasted the same anymore, after her alightment. And then the smell of acetone lingering in her nostrils, her life shifting down the harsh corridor between two kinds of time. Her appetite gone. She moved the food around her plate and looked at the beautiful young woman across from her.

Rose was animated, laughing, explaining something that Todd had done to anger the staff in the atrium. The woman smiled and laughed too. She could hear the rhythms of the story, even if she couldn't quite sing along. Most of what Rose said was indecipherable. Names, places, responsibilities that the woman had never encountered. But she was in love, and she was alive, and she was excited for Kyle to come home.

Rose offered to grab them dessert from the buffet, and she brought back two scoops of something sweet. The crimson globes thinned into liquid, waxing, waning, melting into happy messy puddles. Rose told another story, or it could have been a word problem, for all the variables. No—it was a joke. What was the punch line?

The woman would probably be on the next voyage home. The point had not been to stay in the suburbs. It had taken every kind of strength to come this far. Only here to see Rose. She might try to find Edward again, but the journey on ground was an unrealistic proposition. She would be lucky to make it back to the planet at all.

Maybe the punch line was that they would never see each other again.

"Look," Rose said.

The construction ship approached the atrium, limbs fanning across the sky. Its corrugated shuttle crowded the area of the window, and the woman gasped, but not because she was afraid. Beyond the metal frame, a profusion of stars and color, ancient events made visible through flickering clouds of light. She could not believe how close it felt, the past, when really it was all impossibly far. Perhaps the opposite was also true. One could locate things long gone, in the vast and willing scenery of the mind.

"Take care of my daughter," the woman said to no one but herself.

Then the ship tilted away. Toward what, she could not guess.

ACKNOWLEDGMENTS

Thank you to my fearless and formidable agent, Monika Woods, who has championed my work since our very first meeting, where we ate the most delicious string beans in midtown. Thank you to my brilliant editor, Gabriella Doob, and to the entire talented team at Ecco, especially Sonya Cheuse, Cordelia Calvert, Aja Pollock, Vivian Rowe, and Lydia Weaver.

My endless thanks and admiration to Denne Michele Norris, Emma Copley Eisenberg, Hernan Diaz, Mary South, Molly McGhee, Ruchika Tomar, and Sasha Fletcher. Your wisdom, generosity, and friendship helped me make a better book. I feel very lucky to know you, and to exist in the same universe as your writing. Thank you to the marvelous Diane Cook and Jessamine Chan for being my role models, and for hand-holding this novel into reality.

For their invaluable support and guidance, thanks to Katie Boland, Dana Spector, Jiah Shin, and Leslie Shipman. Thank you to Yaddo for the gift of time, space, daydreams, and a really fabulous desk, and to the Picador Guest Professorship for giving me the freedom to run away and edit these pages.

Thanks to Chris Beha and *Harper's Magazine* for believing in the short story that eventually became this novel, and for publishing that story with such attention and care.

Thank you to my wonderful mom. Thank you to my family and friends, both here and on the other side of the door. And thank you to Matt, who makes my world bigger every day.